THE MOST EXCITING things to happen in Dullsville in my lifetime, in chronological order:

1. The 3:10 train jumped its tracks, spilling boxes of Tootsie Rolls, which we devoured.

2. A senior flushed a cherry bomb down the toilet, exploding the sewage line, closing school for a week.

3. On my sixteenth birthday a family rumored to be vampires moved into the haunted Mansion on top of Benson Hill!

ALSO BY ELLEN SCHREIBER

VAMPIRE KISSES II: KISSING COFFINS

TEENAGE MERMAID

COMEDY GIRL

Ellen Schreiber

Vampire Kisses

KATHERINE TEGEN BOOKS
HarperTrophy®
An Imprint of HarperCollins*Publishers*

HarperTrophy® is a registered trademark of HarperCollins Publishers Inc.

Vampire Kisses
Copyright © 2003 by Ellen Schreiber
For information address HarperCollins Children's Books,
a division of HarperCollins Publishers, 1350 Avenue of the
Americas, New York, NY 10019.

Library of Congress Cataloging-in-Publication Data
Schreiber, Ellen.
  Vampire kisses / Ellen Schreiber.—1st ed.
    p. cm.
  Summary: Sixteen-year-old Raven, an outcast who always wears
black and hopes to become a vampire some day, falls in love with
the mysterious new boy in town, eager to find out if he can make
her dreams come true.
  ISBN-10: 0-06-009336-6 (pbk.)
  ISBN-13: 978-0-06-009336-5 (pbk.)
  [1. Vampire—Fiction. 2. Interpersonal relations—Fiction. 3.
Gossip—Fiction.] I. Title.
PZ7.S3787Vam 2003   2002155506
[Fic]—dc21   CIP
                                                         AC

❖

First Harper Trophy edition, 2005
Visit us on the World Wide Web!
www.harperteen.com

To my father, Gary Schreiber,
with all my love;
for giving me the wings to fly.

CONTENTS

1	Little Monster	1
2	Dullsville	10
3	Monster Mash	14
4	Truth or Scare	24
5	A Light in the Window	35
6	Exposed	42
7	Happy Halloween	58
8	Looking for Trouble	72
9	Living Hell	77
10	Working Ghoul	89
11	Mission Improbable	98

12 Quitting Time   102

13 A Girl Obsessed   112

14 Hot Pursuit   126

15 Gothic Guest   135

16 Chocolate-and-Vanilla Swirl   159

17 Dream Date   168

18 Movie Madness   179

19 The Snow Ball   194

20 Game Over   218

21 Darkness and Light   230

22 Deadline   251

"I want a relationship
I can finally sink my teeth into."
—Alexander Sterling

I t first happened when I was five.

I had just finished coloring in *My Kindergarten Book*. It was filled with Picasso-like drawings of my mom and dad, an Elmer's-glued, tissue-papered collage, and the answers to questions (favorite color, pets, best friend, etc.) written down by our hundred-year-old teacher, Mrs. Peevish.

My classmates and I were sitting in a semi-circle on the floor in the reading area. "Bradley, what do you want to be when you grow up?" Mrs. Peevish asked after all the other questions had been answered.

"A fire fighter!" he shouted.

"Cindi?"

"Uh . . . a nurse," Cindi Warren whispered meekly.

Mrs. Peevish went through the rest of the class. Police officers. Astronauts. Football players. Finally it was my turn.

"Raven, what do you want to be when you grow up?" Mrs. Peevish asked, her green eyes staring through me.

I said nothing.

"An actress?"

I shook my head.

"A doctor?"

"Nuh, uh," I said.

"A flight attendant?"

"Yuck!" I replied.

"Then what?" she asked, annoyed.

I thought for a moment. "I want to be . . ."

"Yes?"

"I want to be . . . a vampire!" I shouted, to the shock and amazement of Mrs. Peevish and my classmates. For a moment I thought she started to laugh; maybe she really did. The children sitting next to me inched away.

I spent most of my childhood watching others inch away.

I was conceived on my dad's water bed—or on the rooftop of my mom's college dorm under twinkling stars—depending on which one of my parents is telling the story. They were soul mates that couldn't part with the seventies: true love mixed with drugs, some raspberry incense, and the music of the Grateful Dead. A beaded-jeweled, halter-topped, cutoff blue-jeaned, bare-footed girl, intertwined with a long-haired, unshaven, Elton John–spectacled, suntanned, leather-vested, bell-bottomed-and-sandaled guy. I think they're lucky I wasn't more eccentric. I could have wanted to be a beaded-haired hippie werewolf! But somehow I became obsessed with vampires.

Sarah and Paul Madison became more responsible after my entrance into this world—or I'll rephrase it and say my parents were "less glassy eyed." They sold the Volkswagen flower power van that they were living in and actually started renting property. Our hippie apartment was decorated with 3-D glow-in-the-dark flower posters and orange tubes with a Play-Doh substance that moved on its own—lava lamps—that you could stare at forever. It was the best time ever. The three of us laughed and played Chutes and Ladders and squeezed Twinkies between our teeth. We stayed up late, watching Dracula movies, *Dark Shadows* with the infamous Barnabas Collins, and *Batman* on a black-and-white TV we'd received when we opened a bank account. I felt secure under the blanket of midnight, rubbing Mom's growing belly, which made noises like the orange lava lamps. I figured she was going to give birth to more moving Play-Doh.

Everything changed when she gave birth to the playdough—only it wasn't Play-Doh. She gave birth to Nerd Boy! How could she? How could she destroy all the Twinkie nights? Now she went to bed early, and that creation that my parents called "Billy" cried and fussed all night. I was suddenly alone. It was Dracula—the Dracula on TV—that kept me company while Mom slept, Nerd Boy wailed, and Dad changed smelly diapers in the darkness.

And if that wasn't bad enough, suddenly

they sent me to a place that wasn't my apartment, that didn't have wild 3-D flower posters on the walls, but boring collages of kids' handprints. *Who decorates around here?* I wondered. It was overcrowded with Sears catalog girls in frilly dresses and Sears catalog boys in tapered pants and perfectly combed hair. Mom and Dad called it "kindergarten."

"They'll be your friends," my mom reassured me, as I clung to her side for dear life. She waved good-bye and blew me kisses as I stood alone beside the matronly Mrs. Peevish, which was as alone as one can get. I watched my mom walk away with Nerd Boy on her hip as she took him back to the place filled with glow-in-the-dark posters, monster movies, and Twinkies.

Somehow I made it through the day. Cutting and gluing black paper on black paper, finger painting Barbie's lips black, and telling the assistant teacher ghost stories, while the Sears catalog kids ran around like they were all cousins at an all-American family picnic. I was even happy to see Nerd Boy when Mom finally came to pick me up.

That night she found me with my lips

pressed against the TV screen, trying to kiss Christopher Lee in *Horror of Dracula*.

"Raven! What are you doing up so late? You have school tomorrow!"

"What?" I said. The Hostess cherry pie that I had been eating fell to the floor, and my heart fell with it.

"But I thought it was just the one time?" I said, panicked.

"Sweet Raven. You have to go every day!"

Every day? The words echoed inside my head. It was a life sentence!

That night Nerd Boy couldn't hope to compete with my dramatic wailing and crying. As I lay alone in my bed, I prayed for eternal darkness and a sun that never rose.

Unfortunately the next day I awoke to a blinding light and a monster headache.

I longed to be around at least one person that I could connect with. But I couldn't find any, at home or school. At home the lava lamps were replaced with Tiffany-style floor lamps, the glow-in-the-dark posters were covered with Laura Ashley wallpaper, and our grainy black-and-white

TV was upgraded to a twenty-five-inch color model.

At school instead of singing the songs of *Mary Poppins*, I whistled the theme to *The Exorcist*.

Halfway through kindergarten I tried to become a vampire. Trevor Mitchell, a perfectly combed blond with weak blue eyes, was my nemesis from the moment I stared him down when he tried to cut in front of me on the slide. He hated me because I was the only kid who wasn't afraid of him. The kids and teachers kissed up to him because his father owned most of the land their houses sat on. Trevor was in a biting phase, not because he wanted to be a vampire like me, but just because he was mean. He had taken pieces of flesh out of everyone but me. And I was starting to get ticked off!

We were on the playground, standing by the basketball hoop, when I pinched the skin of his puny little arm so hard I thought blood would squirt out. His face turned beet red. I stood motionless and waited. Trevor's body trembled with anger, and his eyes swelled with vengeance as I mischievously smiled back. Then he left his dental impressions in my expectant hand. Mrs.

Peevish was forced to sit him against the school wall, and I happily danced around the playground, waiting to transform into a vampire bat.

"That Raven is an odd one," I overheard Mrs. Peevish saying to another teacher as I skipped past the crying Trevor, who was now throwing a fit against the hard blacktop. I blew him a grateful kiss with my bitten hand.

I wore my wound proudly as I got on the school swing. I could fly now, right? But I'd need something to take me into warp speed. The seat went as high as the top of the fence, but I was aiming for the puffy clouds. The rusty swing started to buckle when I jumped off. I planned to fly across the playground—all the way to a startled Trevor. Instead I plummeted to the muddy earth, doing further damage to my tooth-marked hand. I cried more from the fact that I didn't possess supernatural powers like my heroes on TV than because of my throbbing flesh.

With my bite trapped under ice, Mrs. Peevish sat me against the wall to rest while the spoiled snot-nosed Trevor was now free to play. He blew me a teasing kiss and said, "Thank you." I stuck out my tongue and called him a name I had heard a mobster say in *The Godfather*. Mrs. Peevish immediately sent me inside. I was sent inside a lot during my childhood recesses. I was destined to take a recess from recess.

Dullsville

The official welcome sign to my town should read, "Welcome to Dullsville—bigger than a cave, but small enough to feel claustrophobic!"

A population of 8,000 look-alikes, a weather forecast that's perfectly miserable all year round—sunny—fenced in cookie-cutter houses, and sprawling farmland—that's Dullsville. The 8:10 freight train that runs through town separates the wrong side of the tracks from the right side, the cornfields from the golf course, the tractors from the golf carts. I think the town has it backward. How can land that grows corn and wheat be worth less than land filled with sand traps?

The hundred-year-old courthouse sits on the town square. I haven't gotten into enough trouble to be dragged there—yet. Boutiques, a travel agent, a computer store, a florist, and a second-run movie theater all sit happily around the square.

I wish our house could lie on the railroad tracks, on wheels, and carry us out of town, but we're on the right side near the country club. Dullsville. The only exciting place is an abandoned mansion an exiled baroness built on top of Benson Hill, where she died in isolation.

I have only one friend in Dullsville—a farm girl, Becky Miller, who is more unpopular than I am. I was in third grade when I officially met her. Sitting on the school steps waiting for my mom to pick me up (late as usual) now that she was trying to be a Corporate Cathy, I noticed an impish girl cowering at the bottom of the steps, crying like a baby. She didn't have any friends, since she was shy and lived on the east side of the tracks. She was one of the few farm girls in our school and sat two rows behind me in class.

"What's wrong?" I asked, feeling sorry for her.

"My mom forgot me!" she hollered, her hands covering her pathetic, wet face.

"No, she didn't," I consoled.

"She's never this late!" she cried.

"Maybe she's stuck in traffic."

"You think so?"

"Sure! Or maybe she got a call from one of those nosey sales people that always asks, 'Is your mother home?' "

"Really?"

"Happens all the time. Or maybe she had to stop for snacks, and there was a long line at 7-Eleven."

"Would she do that?"

"Why not, you have to eat, don't you? So never fear. She'll be here."

And sure enough, a blue pickup drove up with one apologetic mother and a friendly, fluffy sheepdog.

"My mom says you can come over Saturday if it's okay with your parents," Becky said, running back to me.

No one had ever invited me to their house

before. I wasn't shy like Becky but I was just as unpopular. I was always late for school because I overslept, I wore sunglasses in class, and I had opinions, all atypical in Dullsville.

Becky had a backyard as big as Transylvania—a great place to hide and play monsters and eat all the fresh apples a growling third-grade stomach could hold. I was the only kid in our class who didn't beat her up, exclude her, or call her names, and I even kicked anyone who tried. She was my three-dimensional shadow. I was her best friend and her bodyguard. And still am.

When I wasn't playing with Becky, I spent my time applying black lipstick and nail polish, scuffing my already-worn combat boots, and burying my head behind Anne Rice novels. I was eleven when our family went to New Orleans for vacation. Mom and Dad wanted to play blackjack on the Flamingo riverboat casino. Nerd Boy wanted to go to the aquarium. But I knew where I was going: I wanted to visit the house of Anne Rice's birth, the historical homes she had restored, and the mansion she now called home.

I stood mesmerized outside its iron gate, a Gothic mega-mansion, my mom (my uninvited chaperone) by my side. I could sense ravens flying overhead, even though there probably weren't any. It was a shame I hadn't come at night—it would have been that much more beautiful. Several girls who looked just like me stood across the street, taking pictures. I wanted to rush over and say, "Be my friends. We can tour the cemeteries together!" It was the first time in my life I felt like I belonged. I was in the city where they stack coffins on top of one another so you can see them, instead of burying them deep within the earth. There were college guys with two-toned spiky blond hair. Funky people were everywhere, except on Bourbon Street, where the tourists looked like they'd flown in from Dullsville. Suddenly a limousine pulled around the corner. The blackest limo I had ever seen. The driver, complete with black chauffeur's hat, opened the door, and she stepped out!

I freaked and watched motionless, like time was standing still. Right before my eyes was my idol of all living idols, Anne Rice!

She glowed like a movie star, a Gothic angel, a heavenly creature. Her long black hair flowed over her shoulders and glistened; she wore a golden headband, a long, flowing silky skirt, and a fabulous vampirish, dark cloak. I was speechless. I thought I might go into shock.

Fortunately my mom's never speechless.

"Could my daughter please have your autograph?"

"Sure," the queen of nocturnal adventures sweetly replied.

I walked toward her, as if my marshmallow legs would melt under the sun at any moment.

After she signed a yellow Post-it note my mom found in her purse, the Gothic starlet and I were standing beside each other, smiling, her arm around my waist.

Anne Rice had agreed to take a picture with me!

I had never smiled like that in my life. She probably smiled like she'd smiled a million times before. A moment she'll never remember, a moment I'll never forget.

Why didn't I tell her I loved her books? Why

didn't I tell her how much she meant to me? That I thought she had a handle on things like no one else did?

I screamed with excitement for the rest of the day, reenacting the scene over and over for my dad and Nerd Boy at our antique-filled, pastel pink bed-and-breakfast. It was our first day in New Orleans, and I was ready to go home. Who cared about a stupid aquarium, the French Quarter, blues bands, and Mardi Gras beads when I'd just seen a vampire angel?

I waited all day to get the film developed, only to find that the picture of me and Anne Rice didn't come out. Sullen, I retreated back to the hotel with my mother. Despite the fact she and I had appeared in photographs separately, could it be possible that the combination of the two vampire-lovers couldn't be captured on film? Or rather it was just a reminder that she was a brilliant bestselling writer, and I was a screamy, dreamy child going through a dark phase. Or maybe it was that my mom was a lousy photographer.

M y Sweet Sixteenth birthday. Shouldn't all
birthdays be sweet? Why should sixteen be
any sweeter? It seemed like a lot of hype to me!

In Dullsville, they celebrate today, my sixteenth birthday, as any other day.

It all started with Nerd Boy's shouting at me.
"Get up, Raven. You don't want to be late. It's
time for school!"

How could two kids come from the same
parents and be so different? Maybe there is
something to that theory about the mailman. But
in Nerd Boy's case my mother must have had an

affair with the librarian.

I dragged myself out of bed and put on a black, cotton sleeveless dress and black hiking boots, and outlined my full lips with black lipstick.

Two white-flowered cakes, one in the shape of a 1 and the other in the shape of a 6, awaited me on the kitchen table.

I grazed the 6 cake with my index finger and licked the icing off.

"Happy birthday!" my mom said, kissing me. "That's for tonight, but you can have this now," she said handing me a package.

"Happy birthday, Rave," my dad said, also giving me a kiss on the cheek.

"I bet you have no idea what you're giving me," I teased my dad as I held the package.

"No. But I'm sure it cost a lot."

I shook the light package in my hand and heard a rattle. I stared at the Happy Birthday wrapping paper. It could be the keys to a car— my very own Batmobile! After all, it was my sixteenth birthday.

"I wanted to buy you something special," my mom said, smiling.

I ripped the package open excitedly and lifted the jewelry box lid. A string of shiny white pearls stared back at me.

"Every girl should have a pearl necklace for special occasions." My mom gleamed.

This was my mom's corporate version of hippie love beads. I forced a crooked smile as I tried to hide my disappointment. "Thanks," I said, hugging them both. I began to put the necklace back in the box, but my parents glared at me, so I reluctantly modeled it for them.

"It looks gorgeous on you." My mom glowed.

"I'll save them for something really special," I replied, putting them back in the box.

The doorbell rang, and Becky came in with a small black gift bag.

"Happy birthday!" she shouted as we went into the living room.

"Thanks. You didn't have to get me anything."

"You say that every year," she teased and handed me the bag. "By the way, I saw a moving van last night outside the Mansion!" she whispered.

"No way! Someone finally moved in?"

"Guess so. But all I saw were the movers carrying in oak desks, grandfather clocks, and huge crates marked 'Soil.' And they have a teenage son."

"He was probably born wearing khaki pants. And I'm sure his parents are some boring Ivy Leaguers," I replied. "I hope they don't remodel it and chase out all the spiders."

"Yeah. And tear down the gate and put up a white picket fence."

"And a plastic goose on the front lawn."

We both giggled like mad as I stuck my hand into the bag.

"I wanted to buy you something special, since you're sixteen."

I pulled out a black leather necklace with a pewter charm. The charm was a bat!

"I love it!" I screamed, putting it on.

My mom leered at me from the kitchen.

"Next time we'll give her money," I heard her tell my father.

"Pearls!" I whispered to Becky as we left the house.

I was in gym class wearing a black shirt, shorts, and combat boots instead of the required white-on-white and gym shoes. *Really, what's the point?* I thought. Does a white ensemble make a student a better athlete?

"Raven, I don't feel like sending you to the office today. Why don't you just give me a break for once and wear what you're supposed to wear?" Mr. Harris, the gym teacher, whined.

"It's my birthday. Maybe you could give *me* a break this once!"

He stared at me, not knowing what to say. "Just today," he finally agreed. "And not because it's your birthday, but because I'm not in the mood to send you to the office."

Becky and I giggled as we went off toward the bleachers where the class was waiting.

Trevor Mitchell, my kindergarten nemesis, and his shuffling sidekick, Matt Wells, followed us. They were perfectly combed, conservative, rich soccer snobs. They knew they were great looking, and it made me sick that they were so cocky.

"Sweet sixteen!" Trevor said, obviously having overheard my chat with Mr. Harris. "How lovely! Just ripe for love, don't you think, Matt?" They were close on our heels.

"Yeah, dude," Matt agreed.

"But maybe there's a reason she doesn't wear white—white is for virgins, right, Raven?"

He was gorgeous, no doubt about it. His blue eyes were beautiful, and his hair looked as perfect as a model's. He had a girl for every day of the week. He was a bad boy, but he was a rich bad boy, which made him very boring.

"Hey, I'm not the one wearing white under-wear, am I?" I asked. "You're right—there's a reason I wear black. Maybe you're the one who oughta get out more."

Becky and I sat on the far end of the bleachers, leaving Trevor and Matt standing on the track.

"So how are you spending your birthday?" Trevor shouted, sitting with the rest of the class, loud enough for everyone to hear. "You and farmer Becky sitting home on a Friday night, watching *Friday the Thirteenth*? Maybe placing some personal ads? 'Sixteen-year-old single white mon-ster girl seeks mate to bond with for eternity.'"

The whole class laughed.

I didn't like it when Trevor teased me, but I liked it even less when he teased Becky.

"No, we were thinking of crashing Matt's party tonight. Otherwise there won't be anyone interesting there."

Everyone was shocked, and Becky rolled her eyes, as if to say, *What are you dragging me into now?* We had never been to one of Matt's highly publicized parties. We were never invited, and we wouldn't have gone if we were. At least I wouldn't.

The whole class waited for Trevor's reaction.

"Sure, you and Igor can come . . . but remember, we drink beer, not blood!" The whole class laughed again, and Trevor high-fived Matt.

Just then Mr. Harris blew his whistle, signaling us to hightail it off the bleachers and run like greyhounds around the track.

But Becky and I walked, indifferent to our sweating classmates.

"We can't go to Matt's party," Becky said. "Who knows what they'll do to us?"

"We'll see what they do. Or what we'll do. It's my Sweet Sixteenth, remember? A birthday to never forget!"

The most exciting things to happen in
Dullsville in my lifetime, in chronological
order:

1. The 3:10 train jumped its tracks, spilling
boxes of Tootsie Rolls, which we devoured.

2. A senior flushed a cherry bomb down the
toilet, exploding the sewage line, closing school
for a week.

3. On my sixteenth birthday a family
rumored to be vampires moved into the haunted
Mansion on top of Benson Hill!

The legend of the Mansion went like this: It

was built by a Romanian baroness who fled her country after a peasant revolt in which her husband and most of his family were killed. The baroness built her new home on Benson Hill to resemble her European estate in every detail, except for the corpses.

She lived with her servants in complete isolation, terrified of strangers and crowds. I was a small child at the time of her death and never met her, although I used to play by her solitary monument in the cemetery. Folks said she would sit by the upstairs window in the evenings staring at the moon, and that even now, when the moon is full, if you look from just the right angle, you can see her ghost sitting in that same window gazing at the sky.

But I never saw her.

The Mansion has been boarded up ever since. Rumor had it there was a witchlike Romanian daughter interested in black magic. In any case, she wasn't interested in Dullsville (smart lady!) and never claimed the place.

The Mansion on Benson Hill was quite gorgeous to me in its Gothic way, but an eyesore to everyone else. It was the biggest house in town—

and the emptiest. My dad says that's because it's in probate. Becky says it's because it's haunted. I think it's because women in this town are afraid of dust.

The Mansion, of course, had always fascinated me. It was my Barbie Dream House, and I climbed the hill many nights hoping to spot a ghost. But I actually went inside only once, when I was twelve. I was hoping I could fix it up and make it my playhouse. I was going to put up a sign that said, NO NERD BOYS ALLOWED. One night I climbed the wrought iron gate and scurried up the winding driveway.

The Mansion was truly magnificent, with vines dripping down its sides like falling tears, chipped paint, shattered roof tiles, and a spooky attic window. The wooden door stood like Godzilla, tall and powerful—and locked. I snuck around the back. All the windows were boarded up with long nails, but I noticed some loose boards hanging over the basement window. I was trying to pull them loose when I heard voices.

I crouched behind some bushes as a gang of high-school seniors stumbled near. Most were drunk and one was scared.

"C'mon, Jack, we've all done it," they lied, pushing a guy wearing a baseball cap toward the Mansion. "Go in and get us a shrunken head!"

I could see Jack Patterson was nervous. He was a handsome crush-worthy guy, the kind who should be spending his time shooting hoops or making girls swoon, not sneaking into haunted houses to win friends.

It was like Jack had already seen a ghost as he approached the Mansion. Suddenly he looked behind the bushes where I was hiding. I gasped and he screamed. I thought we were both going to have a heart attack. I crouched back down, because I heard the gang approaching.

"He's screaming like a little girl and he's not even in yet!" one of them teased.

"Get outta here!" Jack said to the guys. "I'm supposed to do this alone, right?"

He waited for the others to retreat and then nodded to me that it was clear.

"Damn, girl, you scared me! What are you doing here?"

"I live here and lost my keys. I'm just trying

to get back in," I joked.

He caught his breath and smiled. "Who are you?"

"Raven. I already know who you are. You're Jack Patterson. Your father owns the department store where my mom buys her swank purses. I've seen you working the cash register."

"Yeah, I thought you looked familiar."

"So why are you here?"

"It's a dare. My friends think the place is haunted, and I'm supposed to sneak inside and get a souvenir."

"Like an old couch?"

He smiled that same smile. "Yeah, goofball. But it doesn't matter. There's no way—"

"Yes, there is!" And I showed him the loose boards at the basement window.

"You go in first," he said, prodding me forward with trembling hands. "You're smaller."

I slithered easily through the window.

Inside, it was really dark, even for me. I could barely make out the cobwebs. I loved it! There were stacks of cardboard boxes everywhere, and it smelled like a basement that had been there since the beginning of time.

"C'mon already!" I said.

"I can't move! I'm stuck."

"You have to move. Do you want them to find you with your backside hanging out?"

I yanked and pushed and pulled. Finally Jack came through, to my relief, but not his.

I led the terrified senior through the moldy basement. He held on to my hand so tight I thought he would break my fingers.

But it was nice to hold his hand. It was big and strong and masculine. Not like Nerd Boy's, whose tiny hand always felt squishy and smarmy.

"Where are we going?" he whispered in a terrified voice. "I can't see a thing!"

I could make out the shapes of massive chairs and sofas, covered with dusty white cloth, probably once belonging to the old woman who stared at the moon.

"I see some stairs," I said. "Just follow me."

"I'm not going any further! Are you crazy?"

"How about a full-length mirror?" I teased, peeking behind a cloth.

"I'll take one of these empty boxes!"

"That's no good. Your friends will kill you. You'll be a laughingstock the rest of your life.

Believe me, I know how it is."

I looked back at him and saw the terror on his face. I wasn't sure if he was scared of his friends outside or of the basement steps that might cave in at the slightest pressure. Or maybe he was afraid of ghosts.

"Okay," I said. "You wait here."

"Like I could go anywhere? I have no idea how to get back!"

"But first . . ."

"What?"

"Let go of my hand!"

"Oh, yeah."

He let me go. "Raven—"

"What?"

"Be careful!"

I paused. "Jack, do you believe in ghosts?"

"No, of course not!"

"So you don't think there is a ghost here? Of that old woman?"

"Shhh! Don't talk so loud!"

I smiled with expectation. But then I remembered his gang's dare and grabbed his baseball cap. He screamed again.

"Relax, it's just me, not one of those spooky

ghosts you don't believe in."

I carefully ascended the creaky steps and bumped into a closed door at the top. But it opened when I turned the knob. I was in a wide hallway. Moonlight was shining through cracks in the boarded windows. The Mansion seemed even bigger on the inside. I caressed the walls as I walked, the dust softly caking my hands. I turned a corner and stumbled upon a grand staircase. What treasures lay at the top of it? Is that where the ghosts of the baroness appeared?

I tiptoed up the stairs, as mouselike as I could in my heavy combat boots.

The first door was locked, as was the second and third. I leaned my ear to the fourth door, and I heard the sound of faint crying from the other side. A cold chill ran through me. I was in heaven. As I listened closer, I realized it was only the wind whistling through the boarded windows. I opened a closet, which creaked like an old coffin. Maybe I'd find a skeleton! The only thing I discovered, however, were several old hangers sporting cobwebs instead of clothes. I wondered where the ghosts were. I peered into the library. An open book lay on a small table, as if the woman who stared at the moon had been reading it when she died.

I grabbed *Romanian Castles* off the shelf, hoping it would open a secret passageway into a spook-filled dungeon. Nothing moved except a hairy brown spider that scooted across the dusty shelf.

But the next moment, I heard a loud sound and nearly jumped through the roof—it was the honking of a horn! Startled, I dropped the book. I had totally forgotten about Jack's gang and my new mission.

I ran back down the grand staircase, leaping over the last steps. A bright light was beaming through the boarded-up windows in the living room. I climbed onto the bay window and peered out, safely hidden behind the boards. I could see the seniors sitting on the hood of their car, the headlights shining up through the gate of the Mansion.

One of them was looking in my direction, so I pushed Jack's cap out through an opening between the boards and waved it like I had just landed on the moon. I felt triumphant. The seniors gave the thumbs up in reply.

I found Jack in a sweat, sitting in a corner of the basement on top of some wooden crates. He must have been thinking about rats as well as ghosts.

He grabbed me like a child grabs his mother. "What took you so long?"

I replaced the cap on his head. "You'll need this."

"What did you do with it?"

"I let them know you made it in okay. Ready?"

"Ready!" And he pulled me back through the window like the place was on fire. I noticed he didn't get stuck this time.

We shoved the board back in place. It looked as if we had never been there. "We don't want this to be easy for anyone else," I said.

He stared back like he didn't know what to make of me, or how to thank me.

"Wait! I didn't get a souvenir!" he realized.

"I'll go back in."

"No way!" he said, grabbing my arm.

I thought for a moment.

"Here, take this." I gave him my necklace. A black leather band with an onyx medallion. "It only cost three dollars, but it looks like it was owned by a baroness. Just don't let anyone appraise it."

"But you did all the work, and I'll get all the credit."

"Take it before I change my mind."

"Thanks!"

He weighed the necklace in his hand and gave me a warm kiss on my cheek. I hid behind the crumbling gazebo as he ran back down to his buddies, dangling the necklace in front of their faces, getting high fives. They adored him now and so did I. I held my filthy hand against my freshly kissed cheek.

After that day Jack hung out with the cool club and even became class president. From time to time, I'd see him around the town square, and he'd always have a huge smile for me.

I didn't have a chance to return to my Barbie Dream House. Word spread that Jack had snuck into the Mansion. Fearful that more kids might break in, police patrolled the area at night. It would be years till I visited the Mansion again.

Still sweaty from gym class, Becky and I passed the Mansion on our way home. I noticed something I had never seen before: a light in the window. Windows—they weren't boarded up anymore!

"Becky, look!" I screamed with excitement. This was the best birthday present of all! There was a figure standing in the attic window, staring up at the stars.

"Oh, no! It's true, Raven. There are ghosts!" she screamed, clutching onto my arm.

"Well, this ghost drives a black Mercedes!" I said, pointing to the snazzy car parked in the driveway.

"Let's go," she pleaded.

Suddenly the attic light went out.

We both gasped at the same time. Becky's nails dug into my thrift-store sweater. We waited, wide-eyed and speechless.

"C'mon, let's go!" Becky said.

I didn't move.

"Raven, I'm already late for dinner! We'll be doubly late for Matt's party."

"You've got the hots for ol' Mattie?" I teased, my eyes glued to the Mansion.

But when she didn't reply, I turned to face her. Becky's cheeks were flushed.

"You do!" I said with a gasp. "And you think *I'm* weird!" I declared, shaking my head.

"Raven, I've got to go!"

I would have waited till morning, but whoever was inside wasn't coming out.

The light in the attic window had lit a fire in my soul.

"I saw a Mercedes parked at the Mansion!" I informed my family at dinner. I was late as usual, this time for my own birthday dinner.

"I heard they looked like the Addams Family," Nerd Boy said.

"Maybe they have a daughter your age. Someone who doesn't like to get into trouble," my mother added.

"Then I'd have no use for her."

"Maybe she has a father I can play tennis with," my father said hopefully.

"Whoever it is will need to get rid of all those old mirrors and crates," I added, not realizing what I had said.

They all looked at me. "What crates?" my mom asked. "Don't tell me you've snuck into that house!"

"It's just something I heard."

"Raven!" my mother said in that disapproving mother tone.

It seemed no one in Dullsville had seen the new owners. It was wonderful to have a mystery in this town for a change. Everyone already knew most everything that happened in Dullsville, and most of it wasn't worth knowing.

Matt Wells lived on the good side of town, at the edge of Oakley Woods. Becky and I arrived late and entered the party like we were movie stars entering a premiere. Or rather I did. Poor Becky hung tightly to my side like she was visiting the dentist.

"It'll be okay," I reassured her. "It's a party!"

But I knew why she was nervous. We were subjecting ourselves to ridicule when we could have been safely at home watching TV like Trevor said. But why should the snobs have all the fun? Just because Matt's bedroom was the size of my living room? Just because we didn't wear clothes that were "in"? So that meant I should sit home on my sixteenth birthday?

I felt like Moses parting the Red Sea, as a crowd of snobs dispersed from the hallway upon our entry. Our classmates eyeballed me, decked out in my usual Gothic garb. Too bad Tommy Hilfiger wasn't there. He'd have been flattered. Everyone was wearing his clothes like a school uniform. The sound of Aerosmith rocked throughout Matt's living room. A thick layer of smoke hung above the couches, and the smell of beer permeated the air like cheap incense. Couples who weren't staring disapprovingly at us were staring adoringly at each other. It was going to be useless to try to talk to anyone.

"I can't believe you showed up," Matt said, spotting us in the hallway. "I'd take a picture, but I don't know if you'd be visible!" Yet despite his bark, Matt wasn't as cruel as Trevor. "Beers are out back," he then said. "Want me to show you the way?"

Becky was in awe of Matt. She shook her head and locked herself in the hallway bathroom. Matt laughed and headed for the kitchen. I waited in the living room by a concert-sized speaker, perusing the CDs. Michael Bolton, Celine Dion, and a bunch of show tunes. I wasn't surprised.

I went back to check on Becky and found the bathroom door open. She wasn't in the hallway, so I walked through the crowd of hammered classmates to the kitchen. A group of hundred-dollar-hairstyle girls glared at me and left, leaving me alone. Or so I thought.

"Hey, sexy Monster Chick," a voice said behind me. It was Trevor.

He was leaning against the wall next to me, a can of Budweiser dangling from his hand.

"Does that line work for you at every party?"

He smiled a seductive smile. "I've never kissed a girl with black lips before."

"You've never kissed a girl before," I said and walked past him.

He grabbed my arm and pulled me back to him. He looked at me with his blue eyes and kissed me on the mouth! I have to admit, he was a great kisser, and it didn't hurt that he was gorgeous.

Trevor Mitchell had never even touched me, much less kissed me, except when he bit me in kindergarten. The most I ever got was a thump on the head when I walked too close to him. He had to be drunk. Maybe it was a joke—maybe he was just trying to mess with me. But the way his lips felt against mine, it seemed like we were both enjoying it. I didn't know what to think as he pulled me out the back door, past an inebriated couple mashing on the steps, past garbage cans and the fountain, under tall trees and darkness.

"Are you scared of the dark, Monster Girl?" The woods let so little light in, it was hard to make out the red stripes on his sweater.

"No, I quite like it."

He pushed me up against a tree and started kissing me for real. His hands were everywhere—on me, on the tree.

"I've always wanted to kiss a vampire!" he said, coming up for air.

"I've always wanted to kiss a Neanderthal."

He laughed and went on kissing me.

"So does this mean we're going together?" I asked. Now I was the one coming up for air.

"What?"

"Like when we go to school? We'll hold hands in the halls and hang out together at lunch? See movies on the weekends?"

"Yeah, whatever."

"Then we're going together?"

"Yeah." He laughed. "You can watch me play soccer, and I can watch you turn into a bat." He began softly biting me on the neck. "I bet you like it like this, don't you, Monster Girl?"

My heart sank. Of course, I didn't really want to be Trevor's girlfriend. It's not like he was Mars and I was Venus—we weren't even from the same universe! And I didn't even like him, really. I knew why he'd brought me out here, I knew what he wanted to do, and I knew who he was going to tell. And at the end of it all, he might win ten dollars from all his betting buddies for "getting the Goth Chick." I had hoped he was going to prove me wrong. Instead, he was proving me right.

It was time to get down to business. "Wanna see why I don't wear white? Wanna fly with me?"

"Yeah." He smiled, sort of startled, but very eager. "I bet you fly like Supergirl!"

I urged him over the picket fence into the woods. I could obviously see better than he. My nocturnal habits had always made me a great observer in the dark. Not as good as a cat, but close. I felt safe and secure, with the beautiful moon now guiding me. I looked up and saw several bats fluttering over the trees. I'd never seen bats in Dullsville. But I didn't go to that many parties, either.

"I can't see," Trevor said, removing a branch from his hair.

As we walked on, he flailed his arms like he was going to hit something. Some people are violent drunks; some are slobbering drunks. But Trevor was a terrified drunk. He was really becoming quite unattractive.

"Let's stop here," he said.

"No, just a little bit further," I said, following the bats as they flew into the woods. "It's my sixteenth birthday. I want this to be a night I'll never forget! We need total privacy."

"This is plenty private," he said, groping around and trying to kiss me.

"We're almost there," I said, tugging him on. The lights from the house could no longer be seen, and we couldn't walk five steps without hitting a tree.

"This is perfect!" I finally said.

He squeezed me hard, not because he loved me, but because he was afraid. It was pathetic.

There was a gentle wind blowing through the trees, and the smell of autumn leaves. I heard bats chirping high overhead. The full moon illuminated their wings. It would have been romantic, if only I had had a real boyfriend with me.

Trevor was completely blind in the darkness, feeling everything with his hands and lips. He kissed me all over my face and touched the small of my back. Even blind, it didn't take him long to find the buttons on my shirt.

"No, you first," I told him.

I lifted off his sweater, as unclumsily as I could. I had never done this before. He was wearing a V-neck T-shirt underneath and an undershirt underneath that. *This is going to take forever*, I thought.

I felt his naked chest. Why not? It was right in front of me. It was soft and smooth and muscular.

He pulled me closer, my lacy black rayon shirt touching his naked torso.

"Now you, baby. I want you so bad," he said, straight out of some skin flick on cable.

"Me too, baby." I sighed, rolling my eyes.

I leaned him down slowly on the damp earth. I slid off his loafers and socks. He eagerly took off the rest.

He lay propped up on his arms, completely naked. I stared down at him in the faint moonlight, savoring the moment. How many girls had Mr. Gorgeous laid out by a tree, only to cast them aside the next day? I wasn't the first and I wasn't going to be the last. I was just going to be different.

"Hurry up—come over here," he said. "I'm cold!"

"I'll just be a minute. I don't want you to see me undress."

"I can't see you! I can't even see my own hands!"

"Well, just hang on."

I had Trevor Mitchell's clothes in my arms. His sweater, V-neck, undershirt, khakis, socks, loafers, and underwear. I had his power. His mask. I had his whole life. What was a girl to do?

This girl ran. I ran so hard, like I had never run before. Like I had been training every day in gym class. If Mr. Harris could have seen me then, he surely would have put me on the track team.

The bats flew off, too, as if they were in sync with my movements. I quickly reached the house, Trevor's ensemble wadded in my arms. The snobs drinking on the back porch were too busy talking about their shallow lives to notice me emptying a trash bag half filled with beer cans and stuffing in Trevor's clothes.

I carried the bag into the house and grabbed a startled Becky by the arm. She was delivering beer to a table of poker players.

"Where were you?" she screamed. "I couldn't find you anywhere! I was forced to wait on these creeps! Back and forth—beer, chips, beer, chips. And now cigars! Raven, where am I supposed to get cigars?"

"Forget about cigars! We've gotta run!"

"Hey, toots, where are those pretzels?" a drunken jock demanded.

"The bar is closed!" I said in his face. "Great service demands a great tip!" I grabbed his poker earnings and stuffed them into Becky's purse. "Time to go!" I said, pulling her away.

"What's in the bag?" she asked.

"Trash, what else?"

I pushed her out the front door. The nice thing about not having friends was there was no one to say good-bye to. "What happened?" she kept asking as I pulled her across the front yard. Her ten-year-old pickup truck sat at the end of the street, waiting for us like home base. "Where were you, Raven? You have leaves in your hair."

I waited until we were halfway home before I turned to her with a huge grin and shouted, "I screwed Trevor Mitchell!"

"You did what?" she shouted back, almost swerving off the road. "With who?"

"I screwed Trevor Mitchell."

"You didn't! You couldn't! You wouldn't!"

"No, I mean figuratively. I screwed him so bad, Becky, and I have the clothes to prove it!" And I pulled them out of the trash bag one by one.

We laughed and shrieked as Becky turned a corner near Benson Hill.

Somehow Trevor would find his way out of the darkness. But he wouldn't have his rich threads to mask himself. He'd be naked, cold, alone. Exposed for who he really was.

I would remember my Sweet Sixteenth birthday for the rest of my life and now Trevor Mitchell would, too.

As we drove along the desolate country road that twisted around Benson Hill, the headlights shone against the creepy trees. Moths attacked the windshield as if warning us to choose another way.

"The Mansion's totally dark," I said as we approached it. "Wanna stop for a look-see?"

"Your birthday's over," Becky said in an exhausted voice, keeping her foot on the gas pedal. "We'll go next year."

Suddenly the headlights illuminated a figure standing in the middle of the road.

"Watch out!" I yelled.

A guy with moonlight-white skin and spikey black hair, clothed in a black coat, black jeans, and black Doc Martens, quickly raised his arm to shield his eyes—seemingly from the glare of the headlights rather than the imminent impact of Becky's pickup.

Becky slammed her brakes. We heard a *thud*.

"Are you okay?" she cried.

"Yes. Are you?"

"Did I hit him?" she yelled, panicking.

"I don't know."

"I can't look," she said, hiding her head on the steering wheel. "I can't!" She started to cry.

I jumped out of the truck and anxiously peered around the front, afraid of what I might find lying in the road.

But I saw nothing.

I checked underneath the truck and looked for dents. On closer inspection, I noticed blood splattered on the fender.

"Are you okay?" I called out.

But there was no response.

I grabbed a flashlight from Becky's glove compartment.

"What are you doing?" she asked, worried.

"Searching."

"For what?"

"There was some blood—"

"Blood?" Becky cried. "I've killed someone!"

"Calm down. It could have been a deer."

"A deer doesn't wear black jeans! I'm calling nine-one-one."

"Go ahead—but where's the body?" I reasoned. "You weren't going fast enough to catapult him into the woods."

"Maybe he's under the truck!"

"I already looked. You probably just bumped him and he took off. But I want to make sure."

Becky grabbed my arm, digging her nails into my flesh. "Raven, don't go! Let's get out of here! I'm calling nine-one-one!"

"Lock the door if you have to," I said, tearing myself free. "But keep the engine and the lights on."

"Raven, tell me this . . ." Becky exclaimed breathlessly, gazing at me with terrified eyes. "What normal guy would be walking in the middle of a pitch-black road? Do you think he might be a—?"

I felt the pleasant tingle of goosebumps on my arms.

"Becky, don't get my hopes up!"

I combed the bushes that went down to the creek. Then I headed for the hillside leading up toward the Mansion.

I let out a shriek.

"What is it?" Becky cried, rolling down the window.

Blood! Thick puddles in the grass! But there was no body! I followed the bloodstains, afraid bits of his corpse were strewn everywhere. And then I tripped over something hard. I looked down, anticipating a severed head. I apprehensively shone my flashlight on it. It was a dented paint bucket.

"Is he dead?" Becky gasped as I returned to the truck.

"No, but I think you may have killed his can," I said, dangling the bucket in front of her. "What was he doing painting in the middle of the night? And where was he going?"

"It was just paint!" Becky said with a gasp of

relief, hanging up her cell phone and revving the engine. "Let's get out of here!"

"What was that jerk doing walking in the middle of the road at night?" I wondered out loud. "Maybe he was going to paint some graffiti or something."

"Where did he come from? Where could he have gone so fast?" she mumbled back at me.

In the rearview mirror I caught the reflection of the darkened Mansion just in time to see a light go on in the attic window.

6

Exposed

The story of Naked Trevor spread immediately through Dullsville High. Some students said he stumbled into Matt's house in a trash-bag diaper; others said he was found passed out naked on the back lawn. No one had a clue I was involved. Only Trevor Boy knew the real story. Apparently he tried to pass it off to his buddies as an encounter with a cheerleader. Either way, everyone got a laugh.

Trevor left me alone. He wouldn't even make eye contact with me. Gothic Girl had finally gotten the goods on the popular Soccer Snob.

But I didn't want him to accuse me of theft. I had to give his clothes back, right?

First there was the shoe. I think it was the left. I strung it on the outside of my locker. At first no one seemed to notice the hanging loafer. Those who finally did looked at it and walked on. But the next morning it was gone. One person had noticed it. Now it was time for others to take notice besides good ol' Trevor.

The right brown loafer was strung up in the same fashion. But next to it was a sign: MISSING SOMETHING, TREVOR?

This time I heard giggles as students passed. They didn't realize whose locker it was. But they'd soon be catching on.

Each day a sock would hang out, or a T-shirt. I started noticing Snob Girls who would never talk to me suddenly looking over in algebra with smiling approval. They had been Trevor Tree Girls, promised everything, with nothing to show for it. Well, I had plenty to show.

By the time his khaki pants were hung out, complete with grass stains and dirt, everyone knew whose locker it was. Now kids in the hall were grinning at me. Guys weren't exactly asking me out, but I was suddenly popular—in a quiet kind of way.

Except, of course, with Trevor. But I felt safe. Now that everyone knew whose locker it was, he would be the prime suspect if anything happened to me.

But he did make the odd threat.

"I'll kick your ass, Monster," he said one day. He grabbed my jaw in his hands when Becky and I were starting to walk home.

"Combat boots hurt more than loafers, Neanderthal," I shot back. My face was pressed between his hands.

"Let her go," Matt said, pulling him away. I could see even Matt had enjoyed my prank. I'm sure he got tired of the Trevor attitude sometimes. After all, he was stuck being Trevor's best friend.

"You'll never be anything more than a freak!" Trevor shouted. Fortunately Matt pulled him away again. I didn't feel like going to battle after a long day at school.

"You just wait! You just wait!" he called back to me.

"Talk to my lawyer!" I yelled, secretly hoping I wasn't going to need a plastic surgeon instead.

Time for the grand finale. Lots of students were gathered around my locker. I even saw a freshman taking pictures.

It was the climax everyone had been waiting for: Trevor's white Calvin Klein underwear hotglued to my locker. The sign underneath read: WHITE IS FOR VIRGINS, RIGHT TREVOR?

It would be up there for a while. Everyone saw it. I mean everyone!

"Raven, you defaced school property," Principal Smith scolded me later that day. I had been in Principal Smith's office so many times, it was like seeing an old friend.

"Those lockers have been here forever, Frank," I replied. "Maybe it's time you tell the school board we need new ones."

"I don't think you see the seriousness involved here, Raven. You ruined a locker and embarrassed an honors student."

"What honor? Ask your straight-A cheerleaders and half the drill team how many times he's embarrassed them!"

Principal Smith rattled his pencil in frustration.

"We need to get you involved in something,

Raven. Some club you can belong to, something that will help you make friends."

"The chess club have any openings? Or how about the math club?" I asked sarcastically.

"There are other activities."

"Can you guarantee me a spot on the cheerleading squad? Of course, I'd have to wear a black pleated skirt."

"That's one you have to try out for. But I bet you'd be great."

"Obviously honors students, like Trevor, really respect cheerleaders."

"Raven, high school is hard for most kids. That's just the way it is. Even the people who look as though they belong usually don't feel they belong. But you have so much going for you. You're imaginative. You're smart. You'll figure it out. Just don't damage any more lockers while you're trying to find the answers."

"Sure, Frank," I said, taking the detention slip. "See you soon."

"Not too soon, okay, Raven?"

"I'll try not to work you too hard," I said and closed the door.

The next day I noticed something on my locker that I hadn't put up. In black paint was written: RAVEN IS A HORROR!

I smiled. Very clever, Trevor. Very clever. I felt warm inside. It was the first time he had ever complimented me.

7

Happy Halloween

Halloween. My favorite day of the year. The one day of the year that I fit in. It's the only day everyone accepts and compliments me, and I even get rewarded for it by generous neighbors who don't think I'm too old to celebrate—or are more likely too afraid of what my tricks would be.

But this year I decided I really wanted to wear a costume. I shopped in stores I usually never went to and borrowed things from my mom. I strangled my hair into a ponytail and pink barrettes and wore a lusciously soft white cashmere sweater with a pink tennis skirt. I gave myself a healthy glow with some of my mom's base and blush and wore a soft plum lipstick. I even carried my dad's tennis racket. I went around the house saying things like, "Mummy dear, I'll be home after my tennis lesson!"

Nerd Boy didn't recognize me as I passed him in the kitchen. Then his mouth dropped open when he realized it was me and not a neighbor's kid dropping over for sugar.

"I've never seen you look so . . . good," he said, dressed as a baseball player. I thought I was going to be sick right there and then.

My parents wanted to take pictures. Go figure. They were acting as if I was going to the prom. I let them take just one. I figured my dad should finally have a picture of me he could proudly hang at the office.

Becky and I were eating lunch in the cafeteria later that day. Everyone looked at me like I was the new girl. Really, no one recognized me. It was fun at first, then a bit annoying. I got stares when I dressed in black. I got stares when I dressed in white. I couldn't win! Then Trevor came into the cafeteria dressed as Dracula. His hair was slicked back, and he was sporting a black cape. He had plastic fangs and red-hot lips.

He stood with Matt as he glanced all around to find me. He wanted to rub his new look in my face. Matt finally pointed to me and Trevor did a double take. He stared at me long and hard, looked me up and down. I had never seen him gaze at me like that before. It was as if he was in major Crushville, as he checked out my preppy white sweater and healthy glow.

I thought for sure he'd come over and say something stupid, but instead he sat at the opposite side of the cafeteria with his back to me. He even left before I did. I was free of him! But I was wrong. I should have known our truce wouldn't last.

My little pumpkin basket was almost filled with Smarties, Snickers, Mary Janes, Jolly Ranchers, Dubble Bubble gum, and lots of other tasty treats. And most importantly—spider rings and temporary tattoos. Becky and I had walked all over town and now wondered what awaited us at the front door of the mysterious Mansion. We were saving the best house for last.

Apparently so was everyone else.

There was actually a line to the front door. It was like we were at Disney World. Ghouls, punks, bums, Mickey Mouse, Fred Flintstone, and Homer Simpson were all eagerly waiting their turn. And a bunch of coiffed parents who showed up to steal a peek inside. The circus was in town, and everyone had come to look at the freaks.

"He's really creepy," a twelve-year-old Frankenstein remarked to a pint-sized werewolf as they passed us.

Nerd Boy spotted me and Becky as he walked down the driveway.

"It's well worth the wait, Raven. You'll love it! This is my sister!" he proudly said to his geekoid Batman friend, who looked at me with junior crush-boy eyes.

"Did you see any shrunken heads? Or monsters with fangs?" I asked.

"No."

"Then maybe we're wasting our time."

"That old man is really freaky. He looks scary and he isn't even wearing a costume!"

I could see Nerd Boy was trying to bond with

me, since this was the first time he could actually show me off to his friend. But I could also see Nerdo was expecting a verbal body slam.

"Thanks for the info."

"Thanks? Uh . . . yeah . . . of course, Sis."

"I'll see you at home, if you want to trade any candy bars."

Nerd Boy nodded willingly. He smiled and left like he had finally met his long lost sister.

Becky and I eagerly waited our turn. We were last in line, and as Charlie Brown and a witch who were in front of us stepped away with their goods, the door closed. I looked at the S-shaped knocker and wondered if it was the initial of the new owner. When I peered closer, I saw it was a serpent with emerald eyes. I rapped it gently, hoping the Gothic guy would answer. I wanted to ask him if he was the one in the road the other night, and if so, what he had been doing? Most people got their exercise at the gym, not on spooky country roads in the dead of night. But no one answered.

"Let's go," Becky suggested nervously.

"No, we waited forever for this! I'm not turning back until I get some candy. He owes us!"

"I'm tired. We've been out all night. It's probably just some creepy old guy who wants to go to bed. And I do, too."

"We can't leave now."

"I'm going home, Raven."

"I can't believe you're so chicken. C'mon, I thought we were best friends."

"We are. But it's late."

"Okay, okay. I'll call you tomorrow and tell you all about Mister Creepy."

There were enough treaters walking around that I wasn't afraid for mousy Becky. She'd get home safe. But would I?

I stared at the serpent knocker and wondered what stood behind the huge wooden door. Maybe the new owner would pull me inside and hold me captive in his haunted mansion. I could only hope!

I knocked again and waited. And waited.

I knocked again. I banged and banged and banged. My hand was starting to hurt. I dashed around to the side, then I heard the locks coming unlatched and the creaky door open. I quickly ran back up the front steps. And there he was, standing before me: Creepy Man.

He was tall and skinny, his face and hands pale as snow, in sharp contrast to his dark butler's uniform. He had no hair, not like he'd lost it, but like he'd never had any, and bulging green monster eyes. He looked like he had been alive for centuries. I loved him.

"We have no more candy, miss," he said in a deep foreign accent as he peered down at me.

"Really? But you must have something. Some peanut-butter twists? A piece of toast?"

He opened the door, no further than necessary. I couldn't see anything behind him. What did the place look like inside? How had it changed since I had snuck in four years before? And who were "we," and did they look creepy, too? We could all be friends. I felt someone watching, looming, and I tried to step past the doorway.

"Who else lives here?" I asked boldly. "Do you have a son?"

"I don't have any children, miss. And I'm sorry, but we don't have a crumb left." He started to shut the door.

"Wait!" I blurted out and blocked the door open with my shoe. I reached into my pumpkin basket and pulled out a Snickers and a spider ring. "I'd like to welcome you to the neighborhood. This is my favorite candy and my favorite Halloween treat. I hope you like them, too."

He almost didn't smile. But then as I placed the treats in his spidery snow-white fingers, he smiled a creaky, crackly, skinny-toothed smile. Even his bulging eyes seemed to twinkle.

"See you!" I said, dancing down the steps.

I had met the creepy man! Everyone in town could say they had gotten candy from him, but who else could say they had given him a treat?

I spun around on the front lawn and looked back at the grand Mansion. I saw a shadowy figure watching from the attic window. Was it Gothic Guy? I quickly stopped spinning and stared back, but there wasn't anyone there, just the ruffle of a dark curtain.

I had just passed through the iron gate when a ghoulish vampire in a red Camaro drove up to the curb.

"Want a ride, little girl?" Trevor asked. Matt the Farmer sat comfortably behind the wheel.

"My mother told me not to talk to strangers," I said, taking a difficult bite of a Mary Jane. I was not in the mood for a Trevor confrontation.

"I'm not a stranger, babe. Aren't you too old to be trick-or-treating?"

"Aren't you too old to be toilet-papering the town?"

Trevor got out of the car and came over to me. He looked particularly sexy. Of course, I find all vampires sexy, even fake ones.

"What are you supposed to be?" he asked.

"I'm dressed up as a freak, can't you tell?"

He was trying to be cool but was stepping on himself. I was the only girl that had said no to him. The only girl in town he could never have. I had always been a mystery because of the way I dressed and behaved, and now I was standing before him dressed as his perfect dream girl.

"So you're visiting Amityville by yourself?" He stared up at the Mansion. "You're a wicked chick, aren't you?" He glanced down, sending chills through me—he was gorgeous in his Dracula cape.

I said nothing.

"I bet you've never kissed a vampire before," he said, his plastic teeth shining in the moonlight.

"Well, when you see one, let me know," I

said, and started to walk away.

He grabbed my arm.

"Give it a rest, Trevor!"

He pulled me in closer. "Well, I've never kissed a tennis player," he joked.

I laughed, it was such a corny line. He kissed me full on the mouth, his plastic teeth getting in the way. And I let him. Maybe I was still dizzy from spinning on the lawn.

He finally came up for air.

"Well, now you have!" I said, pulling away. "I think Farmer Matt is waiting for you!"

"I didn't get any candy!" he said, fingering my pumpkin basket. He pulled out a Snickers bar.

"Hey, that's my favorite! Take a peanut-butter twist."

He gobbled up the Snickers with his vampire teeth, which came loose and fell on the ground, dripping with chocolate and caramel. I quickly reached for them, but he grabbed my arm, spilling my candy everywhere.

"Look what you've done!" I shouted.

He grabbed handfuls of candy and stuffed them into his jeans. I watched as my remaining treats were strewn across the lawn. The only candy I could salvage were some boring Smarties and a smashed Mars Bar.

"Still want to be an item?" he asked, his pockets stuffed full with my night's work as he pulled me close. "Still want to be my girlfriend?"

Suddenly he let me go and started toward the Mansion. "Now I'll get some real candy."

I grabbed his arm this time. Who knew what Trevor would do if he reached the door?

"Miss me already?" he asked, startled that I hadn't run away.

"They're out of candy."

"Well, I'll just see about that!"

"Their lights are off. They went to sleep."

"This'll wake them up." He pulled out a can of spray paint from underneath his cape. "They definitely need someone who knows how to decorate!"

He walked on toward the Mansion. I ran after him.

"No, Trevor. Don't!"

He pushed past me. He was going to vandalize the one thing in this town that was truly beautiful.

"No!" I cried.

He popped the lid and shook the can.

I tried to pull his arm away, but he threw me down.

"Let's see . . . how about 'Welcome to the neighborhood!'?"

"Don't, Trevor, don't!"

"Or 'Vampires love company!' I'll sign your name."

Not only was he going to deface their property, he was going to frame me for it. He shook the can once more. And began to spray the Mansion.

I rushed to my feet and pulled back my tennis racket. I used to play with my father, and no game was more important to win than this one. I locked my eyes on the aluminum paint-filled cylinder as if it were a ball, and smacked it as hard as I could. The can spun off into the distance, and, like my usual game, I lost my grip and the racket went flying after it. Trevor let out a yell so loud I thought the whole world would hear. I guess I had hit more than the can.

Suddenly the front door light came on, and I heard the jingle of locks being unlatched.

"We gotta get out of here!" I yelled to Trevor, who was crouching down, holding his wounded hand.

I was ready to make my escape when I felt something I had never felt before: a presence. I turned around and let out a soundless gasp, because fear had taken my breath away. I stood frozen.

There he was. Not Creepy Man. Not Mr. or Mrs. Mansion Family. But Gothic Guy, Gothic Mate, Gothic Prince. He stood before me, like a knight of night!

His long black hair lay heavy on his shoulders. His eyes were dark, deep, lovely, lonely, adoringly intelligent, dreamy. A gateway into his dark soul. He, too, stood motionless, breathing me in. His face was pale like mine and his tight black T-shirt was tucked into his black jeans, which were tucked into monster-chic punk-rock combat boots.

Normally fear is something I feel only when I know my mom's hosting a Mary Kay party and wants to use me as a model. But we were on private property, and my curiosity to meet this strange creature was overwhelmed by my terror of being caught.

The tennis shoes really were a good choice tonight. I could hear Trevor yelling at me as he followed me in flight, "You monster! You broke my hand!"

I raced through the open gate and climbed into the waiting Camaro.

"Drive me home!" I screamed. "Now!"

Matt was startled by his unexpected passenger. He just stared at me, in silent denial.

"Drive me now! Or I'll tell the police you were involved!"

"The police?" he blurted out. "What's Trevor got us into now?"

I could see the angry Count Trevor running down the driveway, his cape flowing in the wind. He was almost at the gate. Gothic Guy hadn't moved but continued to stare straight at me.

"Drive! Just drive the freakin' car!" I screamed at the top of my lungs.

The motor started and we peeled away until the Mansion and its unusual occupants were out of view. I turned around and looked out the back window at a shouting Dracula Trevor chasing after us.

"Happy Halloween," I said to Matt as I let out a sigh of relief.

8

Looking for Trouble

I was making my way to history class when I spotted Trevor walking ahead of me. I noticed something unusual about his indoor ensemble— he was wearing a golf glove on his right hand.

"Making a fashion statement?" I teased, catching up to him. "I guess it's a good thing you don't play soccer with your hands!"

He ignored my comments and continued to walk to class.

"Guess you'll have to miss a few sessions of graffiti club," I joked. "Since your trigger finger is out of commission."

He stopped and stared at me coldly. But he thought better of speaking and walked on.

Ouch! I guess I hurt more than his hand.

"I see you made it home safely," I continued, pursuing him. "Matt took great care of me. He's a perfect gentleman!"

But then I realized everything. I had taken away Trevor's pride, his girlfriends, and now had forced his best friend to betray him and side with the enemy. I felt sorry for him . . . almost.

Trevor paused, staring down at me like he was going to explode. But I was distracted by a strange figure talking to the secretary in the principal's office. It was Creepy Man! Standing pale in the bright fluorescent light, his long gray overcoat shrouding his skinny body. And hanging from his pale, bony hand was my dad's tennis racket.

I pulled a fuming Trevor to the wall, where we could safely overhear the conversation.

"What are you doing?" Trevor asked, trying to wriggle away.

"Shhh! That's the butler from the Mansion!" I whispered, pointing.

"So what?"

"He's looking for us!"

"How can he be looking for us? It was dark, stupid!"

"That guy saw us! He probably found the spray cans on the lawn and whatever stuff you sprayed on the wall as proof! And he has my dad's tennis racket!"

"Damn, freak, if you hadn't hit me none of this would have happened."

"If you hadn't been born, none of this would have happened, you creep. Shhh, already!"

"Sir, you can leave the racket with us and we can make an announcement," I heard Mrs. Gerber reply. "What did you say the girl was wearing?"

"A tennis outfit, miss."

"For Halloween?" She laughed and reached for the racket.

But Creepy Man drew back. "I'd prefer to keep it in my possession for now. If you find the owner, she knows where she can claim it. Good day," he said and bowed to a charmed Mrs. Gerber.

I freaked and pulled Trevor behind a statue of Teddy Roosevelt. "It's a trap," I said, squeezing Trevor's gloved hand. "I'll show up and the police will be waiting with handcuffs!"

Students stared at Creepy Man as he walked creepily toward the front doors, glancing around as he left. He was looking for us.

"He's taking the evidence with him, and that evidence is worth two hundred dollars," I whispered to Trevor.

"Yeah, the evidence," he said. "Against you!"

"Me? Your fingerprints were all over it. That guy saw you, too."

"He only saw me running. He could have been after you. You were mad he ran out of candy, so you sprayed his house until he heard you making noise, then you dropped your candy and tennis racket when the lights came on," Trevor said, like he was Sherlock Holmes solving the Case of the Missing Tennis Racket.

"You're going to pin this on me? I can't believe you!"

"Don't worry, I don't think you'll go to jail over this, babe. You'll just get a major spanking by that crazy butler."

I had gotten in enough trouble for things I had done; I didn't want to be punished for things I hadn't done.

Trevor started walking to class.

I caught up to him. "I'll drag you down so bad if anything happens!"

"Who will they believe, freak—an honors student who is a star soccer player or a two-bit gothic chick with one friend, who spends more time in the principal's office than in class?"

"You owe me a tennis racket!" I shouted helplessly as Trevor sauntered off.

I admit it, Trevor had avenged himself for the Naked Woods Night. Because of him I'd lost my dad's fancy-schmancy racket. And more importantly, he'd made me the enemy in the eyes of the only people in town who might understand me and be my friends. They were my freedom from Dullsville and my connection to humanity, but now because of Trevor, the Mansion would be harder to get into than when it was boarded up.

"**Y**ou what?" my father yelled during dinner after I told him I lost his racket.

"Well, it's not exactly lost. I just don't have it."

"Then get it back if you know where it is."

"That would be impossible right now."

"But I have a game tomorrow!"

"I know, Dad, but you have other rackets." I tried to deflate the power of that one particular racket. Big mistake!

"Others? It's that easy for you? Just go buy another Prince Precision OS racket?"

"I didn't mean that—"

"It's bad enough you deface property at school!"

"I'm sorry, but—"

"Sorry's not good enough this time. Sorry's not going to win me my game tomorrow. My racket is. I can't believe I let you take it out of here in the first place!"

"But, Dad, I'm sure you made mistakes when you were a hippie teenager!"

"And I paid for them! Like you're going to pay for my racket."

My bank account had about five dollars in it, the remains of my Sweet Sixteenth birthday money. And I still owed Premiere Video twenty-five dollars in late fees. I quickly did the math in my head. Dad was going to have to keep my allowance until I was thirty.

Then he said the three words that reverberated in my head and made me go dizzy with fury. As he said them I thought I was going to explode into a million unhappy pieces.

"Get a job!" he proclaimed. "It's about time, too. Maybe that'll teach you some responsibility!"

"Can't you just spank me? Or ground me? Or

not speak to me for years like parents do on those talk shows? Please, Dad!"

"It's final! End of story! I'll help you find a job if you can't on your own. But you'll have to do the work yourself."

I ran to my room, wailing like baby Nerd Boy, screaming at the top of my lungs, "You people just don't understand the pressure of being a teenager in my generation!"

As I cried on my bed, I fantasized about sneaking into the Mansion like I did with Jack Patterson when I was twelve and retrieving the racket.

But I also knew I was a little bigger in the hips now and that the window we'd used had been replaced. I'm sure the new owners also had a security system and, in any case, where would I look for the racket with so many rooms and closets? And while I was searching frantically, I was sure to be caught by Creepy Man wielding a gun or some medieval torture device. A part-time job was a less menacing scenario, but not by much.

At this point I really wished I were a vampire—I'd never heard of Dracula's having a job.

Connections. They'd be wonderful if my dad knew Steven Spielberg or the Queen of England, but Janice Armstrong of Armstrong Travel just doesn't cut it for me.

Far worse than having to show up there after school three days a week, answering phones in a perky voice, photocopying tickets with that hideous blinding flash in my eyes, and talking to yuppies going to Europe for the fourth time was the totally conservative dress code.

"I'm sorry, but you won't be able to wear those . . ." Janice began, staring at my shoes. "What do you kids call them?"

"Combat boots."

"We aren't the army. And it's okay to wear lipstick, but it should be red."

"Red?"

"But you can pick any shade."

Very generous, Janice! "How about pink?"

"Pink would be great. And you'll need to wear skirts. But not too short."

"Red skirts?" I asked.

"No, they don't have to be red. They can be green or blue."

"I can pick any shade?" If she was going to

make me feel like an idiot, I was going to act like one.

"Certainly. And hose—"

"Not black?"

"Not ripped."

"And the nail polish," she began, staring at my fingertips.

"Not black, but any shade of red. Or pink would be great," I recited.

"Very good," she said with a big smile. "You're fitting in already!"

"Thanks, I guess," I said as I got up to leave. I checked my watch. The interview had taken fifteen minutes, but it felt like an hour. This job was going to be complete torture.

"I'll see you tomorrow, at four o'clock then, Raven. Any questions?"

"Do I get paid for the interview?"

"You're father said you were bright, but he didn't mention your wonderful sense of humor. We'll get along great. Who knows, you may want to be a travel agent when you get older."

Mrs. Peevish, my infamous kindergarten teacher, would have been proud.

"I already know what I want to be," I replied.

I wanted to say a vampire, just for old time's sake. But I knew she wouldn't get it.

"What do you want to be?"

"A professional tennis player. They get free rackets!"

My mother bought me some horrible brightly colored Corporate Cathy gear so I could fit neatly into the package of Dullsville's business world. I pulled them out of the shopping bags and freaked when I saw the price tags.

"Yikes! These outfits cost more than the tennis racket. Just keep them and we'll be even."

"That's not the point!"

"This doesn't make sense."

I reluctantly modeled a white blouse and blue knee-length skirt. My mother looked at me like I was the daughter she always wanted.

"Don't you remember wearing halter tops, braids, and bell-bottoms?" I asked. "What I wear isn't that much different for my generation."

"I'm not that little girl anymore, Raven. And besides, I never wore lipstick. I went *au naturel*."

"Ugh," I said, and rolled my eyes.

"Being a teenager is hard, I know. But you'll

eventually find out who you really are."

"I know who I am! And working at a travel agency and wearing a white blouse and hose isn't going to make me find the 'inner me.'"

"Oh, sweetie." She tried to hug me. "When you're a teenager, you think that no one understands you and the whole world is against you."

"No, it's just this town that's against me. I'd go crazy, Mom, if I thought the whole world was against me!"

She hugged me hard and this time I let her. "I love you, Raven," she said, like only a smooshy mom can. "You're beautiful in black, but you're smashing in red!"

"Quit it, Mom, you're wrinkling my new blouse."

"I thought you'd never say that!" she said and squeezed me even tighter.

The part-time after-school gig had to go. How could I get the scoop on the Mansion family if I was going to be at work all afternoon? I had to drag all those dry-clean only clothes with me to school and keep them neatly in my locker until school was over. My new afternoon punishment tore me up inside.

"Why doesn't that guy go to school?" I asked Becky as I was getting dressed.

"Maybe he isn't registered yet."

"If I didn't have this stupid job, we could go investigate right now. Ugh!"

I was envious of Becky because she got to go home to the land of cable TV and microwave popcorn, while I went from a school desk to a reception desk.

After parting ways with Becky, I snuck into the restroom and wiped off my black lipstick with a wet paper towel and replaced it with some ultra-flashy shade of red. I truly looked like a ghost with my pale complexion. I reluctantly put on my bright red rayon-and-cotton blends. "I'll miss you, but we'll be back together in a few hours," I said to my black dress and combat boots, placing them in my backpack.

I gave myself a once over—this was one time I really thought being a vampire would come in handy. Maybe I'd look in the mirror and see nothing. Instead I saw a miserable girl standing awkwardly in her red rayon outfit.

I slithered out of the restroom looking right

and left like I was crossing the street and made my escape safely out the front door. Or so I thought.

Trevor was standing on the front steps.

I freaked when I saw him but tried to ignore his presence and move on. I wanted to run, but I wasn't used to skinny heels.

"Hey, Halloween's over!" he shouted, following me. "Where's your tennis skirt? Going to some costume party as Suzie Secretary?"

I continued to ignore him, but he grabbed my arm.

I couldn't let him know that I was working, or where I was working, and, most of all, that I was working because I had to pay my father back for the tennis racket Trevor had made me lose. It would have brought him too much joy.

He looked me over, that same look he had given me when he first saw me in my tennis outfit. This time I was his corporate dream girl.

"So, where are you going?"

"None of your business!"

"Really? I didn't think we kept secrets from each other."

"Get lost already."

"I'll just walk with you then."

I stopped. "You will not walk with me! You will not go anywhere with me! You will leave me alone! For good. Forever!"

"You don't seem your usual loving self," he said, laughing. "Having a bad hair day? You should be used to that by now."

"Trevor, it's over. Your games and mine! You don't have to harass me anymore. We're even. We're even for all of eternity. Okay? So just get out of my face!"

He ran after me when I stormed off.

"Are we breaking up? I didn't know we were going together, baby. Please don't leave me," he begged, jokingly.

I walked quickly past the school fence and scurried down the sidewalk. I had five minutes to get to Armstrong Travel.

"I can't live without you!" he said sarcastically, catching up. "Are you mad because I never gave you black roses? I'll make it up to you. I'll get you new clothes—from the graveyard." He howled with laughter. "Just don't leave me, babe!"

"Cut it out!" I was fuming. He probably had two hundred dollars in his back pocket and I'd have to work for eons in a place I hated because of his stupid antics.

"Just tell me where you're going!"

"Trevor, quit it! Get out of here! I'll get a restraining order if I have to!"

"Do you have a date?" He wasn't going to give up.

"Go away!"

"You're meeting someone?"

"Buzz off!"

"Do you have an interview? An interview . . . with the vampire?"

"Get out of my face!"

"Are you going to . . . work?"

I stopped. "No! Are you totally crazy? That's so lame!"

"You are! You've got a job!" He danced around. "I'm so proud of you, my little gothic baby has found herself a job!"

I was fuming inside.

"Trying to better your life? Or are you paying Daddy back for that fancy little tennis racket?"

I was ready to hit him and this time send his head flying off into the distance instead of a can of spray paint.

Just then Matt pulled up. "Trevor, dude. You said you'd be on the steps. I don't have time to drive all over town trying to find you. We have to go."

"Good, your baby-sitter found you," I said.

"I'd offer you a ride to work, but we have places to be," Trevor teased.

As the Camaro whizzed off I looked at my watch. Great! My first day of work and I was late.

Big Ben, the Eiffel Tower, and a Hawaiian sunset loomed behind the reception desk at Armstrong Travel, a constant reminder that there was life outside Dullsville, and that excitement was very far away.

The only thing exciting about working at Armstrong's was the gossip. Under normal circumstances, I found the scandals of the town quite boring—the mayor seen cavorting with a Vegas showgirl, a local TV reporter from WGYS faking an alien abduction story, a Brownie leader embezzling earnings from the cookie bake-off.

But now life was different—there have been Mansion family sightings!

Ruby, the perky partner, filled me in on all the latest. She's like a walking *National Enquirer*.

"It's still a mystery what the husband does"—referring to the Mansion family—"but he's obviously wealthy. The butler does the grocery shopping at Wexley's on Saturday at exactly eight o'clock P.M. and picks up the dry cleaning on Tuesdays—all dark suits and cloaks. The wife is a tall pale woman in her mid-forties with long dark hair and she always wears dark sunglasses."

"It's like they're vampires," Ruby concluded, not knowing about my fascination. "They've only been seen at night; they look so ghoulish, dark, and brooding, like they're straight out of a B-movie horror flick. And no visitors have been inside that house. Not one. Do you think they're hiding something?"

I was hanging on Ruby's every word.

"They've lived there for over a month," she continued, "and haven't painted the place, or even cut the grass! They've probably even added creaky doors!"

Janice laughed out loud and ignored her

ringing phone. "Marcy Jacobs was saying the same thing," Janice added. "Can you imagine? Not mowing your lawn or planting flowers. Don't they wonder what the neighbors think?"

"Maybe they don't care what the neighbors think. Maybe they like it that way," I interjected.

They both looked at me in horror.

"But get this," Ruby said. "I heard that the wife was at Georgio's Italian Bistro and ordered Henry's special antipasto . . . without garlic! That's what Natalie Mitchell says her son said."

So? I thought. *I like a full moon. Does that make me a werewolf? Big deal. And who can trust Trevor and his family?* The buzzing of the front door brought the gossip session to a complete halt. And the new customer made us all buzz.

It was Creepy Man!

"I have to finish something in the back!" I whispered to Ruby, whose eyes were riveted to the bony man.

I scurried as fast as I could, not looking back until I was safely standing behind the Xerox machine. Yet I yearned to run to good ol' Creepy, squeeze his fragile body and tell him I was sorry for the Trevor Halloween paint job. I wanted to listen to all he had to say about the world as he knew it, his adventures and travels. But I couldn't, so I cowered behind the copy machine and copied my hand.

"I'd like two tickets to Bucharest," I heard him say, taking a seat at Ruby's desk.

I craned my neck to see him.

"Bucharest?" Ruby asked.

"Yes, Bucharest, Romania."

"And when would you be going?"

"I'm not going, madam. The tickets are for Mr. and Mrs. Sterling. They would like to depart on November first, for three months."

Ruby fiddled with her computer. "Two seats . . . in economy?"

"No, first-class please. Just as long as the flight attendants serve them some bloody wine, the Sterlings are always happy!" he said in his thick accent, laughing.

Ruby laughed back awkwardly, and I chuckled inside.

She went over the itinerary and handed him a copy.

"It's like giving blood, the cost of tickets these days!" Creepy Man laughed, signing.

This was getting good!

Ruby swiped his credit card. "And you're not going, sir?" she asked, as he signed his name, trying to pull more info out of him. Way to go, Rubes!

"No, the boy and I will stay behind."

Boy? Was he referring to Gothic Guy? Or did the Sterlings have a child I could baby-sit? I could play hide-and-seek with him in the Mansion.

"The Sterlings have a boy?" Ruby asked.

"He doesn't get out much. Stays in his room listening to loud music. That's what they do at seventeen."

Seventeen? Did I hear him right? Seventeen? He was talking about Gothic Guy. But why wasn't he in school?

"He's always had a tutor. Or as you say in this country, he's been home-schooled," Creepy Man answered, as if he had read my mind. Or he should have said, Mansion-schooled! No one was home-schooled in Dullsville.

"Seventeen?" Ruby repeated, trying to pump more information from his brittle bones.

"Yes, seventeen . . . going on one hundred."

"I know how that is," Ruby interjected. "My girl just turned thirteen, and she thinks she knows everything!"

"He acts like he's lived before, if you know what I mean, with all his grand opinions about the world." Creepy Man laughed a maniacal laugh that sent him into a coughing frenzy.

"Can I get you anything else?"

"I'd like a town map."

"Our town?" she asked, with a laugh. "I'm not sure we even have them."

She turned to Janice, who just shook her head.

"There's the main square and the cornfields," Ruby said, rifling through her desk. "Are you sure you don't want a map of somewhere more exciting?" she asked, offering him a map of Greece.

"This is all the excitement a man of my age can handle, thank you," he said with a grin. "The square reminds me of my village in Europe. It's been centuries since I've seen it."

"Centuries?" Ruby asked, curiously. "Then you hide your age well," she teased.

If anyone could get info on the walking dead, it was Ruby. She could flirt with the best of them.

Creepy Man's face turned from a white wine to a bright burgundy.

"You are so kind, dear," he said, tapping his bald head with a red silk handkerchief. "Thank you for your time," he said, preparing to leave. "It's been lovely, and you have been lovely, too." He grabbed her hand in his bony fingers and smiled a crackling smile.

As he stood up, he looked directly at me and through me like he knew he had seen me before. I could feel his cold stare as I frantically turned around, quickly gathering together the thirteen copies of my hand.

I didn't dare turn back around until I heard the door close. I peered out as he walked past the front window—and he glanced back like he was looking straight through me. I felt a chill go through my body. I loved it.

The rest of the day whizzed by. I hardly noticed it was after six.

I slung my black bag over my shoulder.

"Wow, we'll have to pay you for overtime!" Ruby said, as I got up from the reception desk.

If I couldn't be Elvira or the Bride of Dracula, I'd be Ruby. She was the complete opposite of me in her white-on-white—white go-go boots with a tight white vinyl dress, or a smart white pants suit with white heels. She wore bob-length white-blond hair and always touched up her make-up with a white compact that bore an R made of red rhinestones. She even had a white poodle that she sometimes brought to the agency. She always had boyfriends coming in to visit. They knew she was major class.

I approached her desk, which was covered with white crystals, white angel ornaments, and a smiling thirteen-year-old girl framed in white Lucite.

"Ruby?" I asked as she fiddled with her white leather purse.

"What, honey?"

"I was just wondering?" I said, twisting my purse strap. "Do you . . ."

"What is it, dear? Sit down." She grabbed Janice's chair and wheeled it next to hers.

"About today . . . I know this sounds crazy, but do you . . . well . . . do you believe in . . . vampires?"

"Do I?" She laughed, fingering her crystal necklace. "I believe in a lot of things, honey."

"But do you believe in vampires?"

"No!"

"Oh." I tried not to show my disappointment.

"But what do I know?" she chuckled. "My sister, Kate, swears she saw the ghost of an old farmer in a cornfield when we were kids. And I dated this guy who saw something silver shoot straight up in the sky, and my best friend, Evelyn, swears numerology helped her find a husband, and my chiropractor heals people by putting magnets on their joints. What's fantasy for some is reality for others."

I hung on her every word.

"So do I believe in vampires?" she continued. "No. But I also didn't believe Rock Hudson was gay. So what do I know?" She smiled a sparkling white smile.

I laughed as I walked to the door.

"Raven?"

"Yes?"

"What do you believe in?"

"I believe in—finding out!"

11

Mission Improbable

"I'm on a mission!" I screamed to Becky, who was already waiting on the swings in Evans Park. I had told her to meet me at seven P.M. "You'll never believe what's happening!"

"You have another pair of Trevor's underwear?"

"Trevor who? No, this is way beyond him! Way beyond the city limits. This is totally out of this world!"

"What gives?"

"I have all the dirt on the Mansion family!"

"Oh, the vampires?"

"You know?"

"It's all over town. Some say it's the way they dress. Some say they're just weird. Mr. Mitchell told my father they must be inhuman since they ate at Georgio's and held the garlic."

"But that's the Mitchells. Still, I may have to add that to my journal. Every bit of info is crucial!"

"Is this why we're meeting?"

"Becky, do you . . . believe in vampires?"

"No."

"No?"

"No!"

"That's it? You're not even going to think about it?"

"You could have asked me that on the phone. I cut out early on a second helping of macaroni and cheese!"

"This is of major importance!"

"Are you mad? Do you want me to believe in vampires?"

"Well . . ."

"Raven, do you believe in them?"

"I've wanted to for years. But who knows? I didn't believe Rock Hudson was gay."

"Who's Rock Hudson?"

I rolled my eyes. "Never mind. I asked you to meet me here to help me out on my mission. See, the answers lie not in rumors, but in truths, and the truth lies in that Mansion. And every Saturday night Creepy Butler Man goes to Wexley's for an hour of grocery shopping. I drove by the Mansion, and they don't seem to have a security system. And if I play my cards right, Gothic Guy will be keeping to himself in his attic room of blaring Marilyn Manson angst. He'll never hear me."

"He'll never hear you doing what?"

"Finding the truth."

"This sounds so way out."

"Thank you."

"So you need me to be at my house waiting by the phone, so when you get safely home, you can call me and share all the details?"

I stared at her hard.

"No, I need you to be my lookout."

"You know this is trespassing? Like *really* trespassing? Like breaking and entering?"

"Well, if I can find an open window, then I won't be breaking. I'll only be entering. And if it all goes as planned, no one will be the wiser and so then I won't even be entering. I won't even get in trouble for exiting!"

"I shouldn't . . ."

"You should."

"I can't."

"You can."

"I won't."

"You will!"

The conversation stopped. "You will!" I said, this time sternly. I hated to be bossy, but it had to be done. I got up from my swing. "I won't steal anything. You'll be an accomplice to nothing. But if I do find out something major, colossal, spectacular, totally out of this world, then we can both share the Nobel Prize."

"We have till Saturday, right?"

"Yes. Which gives me plenty of time to gather more info and comb the Mansion grounds. And you have plenty of time to—"

"Think of excuses?"

I smiled. "No, to finish your macaroni and cheese."

12

Quitting Time

It was better than graduation day: the day my part-time job was over. I had safely cleared $200 after taxes. Enough for dear old dad to buy a sparkling new tennis racket and a new can of bright neon-yellow tennis balls.

I felt a little tinge of melancholy as I picked up my sweater to leave Armstrong Travel, my check safely in my purse. Ruby gave me a huge hug, a real hug, not like Janice's porcelain baby-doll hug.

I waved good-bye to Big Ben, the Eiffel Tower, and the Hawaiian sunset.

"Feel free to come back anytime!" Ruby said. "I'm really going to miss you. You're one of a kind, Raven."

"You are, too!"

She really was, and it was nice to have finally bonded with someone who was different from the average Dullsvillian.

"Some day you'll find a one-of-a-kind guy who is just like you!"

"Thanks, Ruby!"

It was the most tender thing anyone had ever said to me.

Just then Kyle Garrison, Dullsville's golf pro, came in to flirt with Ruby. She had found a lot of one-of-a-kinds for herself. But she deserved it.

I placed my paycheck on my night table, and I curled up in bed, happy that my prison sentence was over and that I could cash the check tomorrow and proudly hand all my earnings over to Dad. But of course I couldn't sleep. I lay awake all night, wondering what my one-of-a-kind guy would look like. I prayed he didn't wear plaid pants like Kyle the golf pro.

Then I thought about the guy at the

Mansion. And wondered if I'd already met my one-of-a-kind.

"What are you so smiley about?" Trevor asked me the next day after lunch. I couldn't help but smile, even to Trevor. I was that happy.

"I'm retired." I beamed. "Now I can just live off the interest!"

"Really? Congratulations. But I got so used to seeing you in your cute secretary outfits. You can wear them just for me now," he said, leaning in close.

"Get off," I yelled, pushing him away. "You're not going to spoil my day!"

"I won't spoil your day," he said, standing back. "I'm proud of you." He smiled a gorgeous smile, but it was mixed with underlying evil. "Now you should have enough money to take me out. I like horror films."

"But they're too scary for children like you. I'll call you in a couple years."

I laughed and walked on. This time he didn't stop me. I guess he really wasn't going to spoil my day after all.

Eighth period was finally over. I quickly went to meet Becky at my locker for an after-school ice cream and Mansion plan update. There was a crowd of students standing around my locker. Becky tried to lead me away, but I pushed past her, through the gawking students.

As I approached, the gawking students stepped back.

I looked at my locker, and my heart fell to the floor. Hanging by rope attached to silver duct tape was my father's Prince tennis racket and a sign that read, GAME OVER! I WIN!

My head started to spin like in *The Exorcist*. Trevor Mitchell had kept the racket the whole time. Could he have somehow gotten it the day Creepy Man came to school?

My body shook with fury. All those ringing phone lines, all those angry customers, all the boring faxes, the sickening taste of envelopes. Watching people fly, drive, and ski their way out of Dullsville as I handed them their tickets to freedom. All because Trevor had been waiting for the right moment to return the racket.

I let out a scream that started in my boots and ended echoing off the walls.

Several startled teachers ran out to see what had happened.

"Raven, are you okay?" Ms. Lenny asked.

I didn't know if the crowd had dispersed or was still hanging on; I only saw the tennis racket. I couldn't breathe, much less speak.

"What happened?" Mr. Burns shouted.

"Are you choking? Do you have asthma?" Ms. Lenny asked.

"Trevor Mitchell—" I began through gritted teeth.

"Yes?"

"He's been beaten up. He's in the hospital!"

"What? How?"

"Where? When?" the panicked teachers inquired alternately.

I took a deep breath. "I don't know how or where!" I turned to them, my body fuming and my head ready to explode. "But I'll tell you this— it'll be soon!"

The puzzled teachers stared back.

I grabbed the tennis racket with all my might, yanking it so hard the duct tape ripped off a band of green paint from my already grungy locker.

I bolted out of school, thirsting for blood.

Students were scattered on the front lawn, waiting for rides. When I didn't find Trevor, I marched around the back.

I spotted him at the bottom of the hill on the soccer field. Waiting for me. He was surrounded by the entire soccer team.

Trevor had planned this. He had patiently waited for this day as I impatiently worked. He knew I'd come after him. He knew I'd be fuming. He knew I'd want to fight. And now he could prove to his buddies that he was king again, that he had gotten Gothic Girl, if not by the tree, then by the racket. And he wanted all his buddies to witness it.

I moved quickly, charged with a bloodthirsty rage. I stormed down the hill to the soccer field, thirteen jocks and one proud antagonist staring at me. Everyone waiting for me to get the bait, and the bait was Trevor.

I pushed past the soccer snobs and walked up to Trevor, clutching my dad's racket, ready for the kill.

"I had it the whole time," he confessed. "I chased that freaky butler dude down that day after school. He wanted to give the racket back himself, but I told him I was your boyfriend. He seemed disappointed."

"You told him you were my boyfriend? Gross!"

"It's grosser for me, babe. You'd be going out with a soccer player. I'd be going out with a freak show!"

I pulled back the racket to take a swing.

"I was going to return it sooner, but you looked so happy going to work."

"You're going to have to wear more than a golf glove when I get through with you this time!"

I swung at him and he jumped back.

"I knew you'd come running after me. Girls always do!" he announced proudly.

His crowd of puppets laughed.

"But you're running after me, too, aren't you, Trevor?"

He stared at me, puzzled.

"It's true," I continued. "Tell your friends! They're all here. But I'm sure they knew it all along. Tell them why you're doing this!"

"What are you talking about, freak?" I could see by his expression he was ready for a battle, but he wasn't expecting to play this kind of game.

"I'm talking about love," I said coyly.

The whole crowd laughed. I had a weapon that was better than any two-hundred-dollar racket: humiliation. To accuse a soccer snob of being attracted to a Gothic girl was one thing, but to use this mushy gushy word in front of a six-teen-year-old macho guy was sure to bring the house down.

"You're really freaking out!" he shouted.

"Don't be so embarrassed. It's rather cute, really," I said smugly and smiled at the goalie. "Trevor Mitchell loves me. Trevor Mitchell loves me!" I sang.

Trevor didn't know what to say.

"You're on drugs, girl," Trevor declared.

"Lame comeback, Trevor." I looked at all his smiling soccer snob friends and then glared at him. "It was so obvious the way you felt, I should have known all along." Then I said in my loudest voice, "Trevor Mitchell, you're in love with me."

"Right, you clown! Like I have a poster of you on my bedroom wall. You're nothing but a skank."

The skank bit hurt, but I let the pain fuel me

for the next round.

"You didn't go to Oakley Woods with a poster. You didn't dress up like a vampire to impress a poster. And you didn't hide my dad's racket so you could gain the attention of a raging poster!"

The soccer guys must have been impressed by my argument, because they didn't attack me or defend Trevor, but instead waited to see what would happen next. "None of your friends here give me the time of day," I went on. "It's 'cause they don't care about me, but you care. You care like crazy. You're telling me the time every day."

"You're crazy! You're nothing but a drugged-up, freaked-out loser girl, and that's all you'll ever be."

Trevor looked at Matt, who only smiled awkwardly and shrugged his shoulders. There were snickers from his other mates and whispered words I couldn't hear.

"You want me so bad," I shouted in his face. "And you can't have me!"

He came at me, everything swinging, and it was a good thing I had my dad's tennis racket to defend myself against his punches. There must have been something pitiful about a furious jock trying to attack a girl, or maybe Trevor's gang of soccer dudes secretly enjoyed seeing him humiliated, because they pulled him back and Matt, along with the goalie, stepped in front of me like a handsome barricade.

Just then Mr. Harris blew his whistle for practice.

There was no time for thank-yous to Matt and the others or "Gee, this has been fun—we'll have to do it again some time." I ran back up the hill triumphantly. I couldn't wait to tell Becky.

Did I really believe Trevor was in love with me? No. It seemed as unlikely as the existence of vampires. Mr. Popular loves Ms. Unpopular. But I had made a good case, and the important thing was, everyone had bought it.

I was finally free.

A Girl Obsessed

Suddenly other Dullsvillians reported Gothic Guy sightings.

"He's really great looking, but a major weird-fest must be going on in that haunted house!" Monica Havers whispered to Josie Kendle in algebra class.

"He actually came out of his dungeon?"

"Yeah, and Trevor Mitchell spotted him coming out of the cemetery at night and said he had blood dripping from his mouth. And when Trevor drove closer, he suddenly disappeared!"

"Really? Hey, you're hanging out with Trevor again?"

"No way! Everyone knows he's in love with that Raven girl. But get this. I saw that ghost guy at the movies last Friday. Alone. Who goes to a movie by himself?"

"Only a loony loser crazy person," Josie said.

"Exactly!"

I rolled my eyes in total disgust.

Then after dinner I was at the 7-Eleven with Becky, picking up soda for my mom, when I noticed a tabloid headline that read, "I Gave Birth to a Two-Headed Vampire Baby."

"Well, it must be true then!" I joked. "Vampires do exist. I read it in the *National Liar*."

Becky and I giggled like little girls.

I turned around and there was Gothic Guy standing right in back of me, staring at the candy bars below the counter.

He was wearing Ray Bans, like a ghostly rock star, and was holding a pack of candles.

"Aren't you the guy—" I whispered breathlessly, as if I had spotted a celebrity.

"Next," the clerk said, summoning him to the counter.

He didn't even notice me. I followed him closely but was edged out by a red-haired fitness queen and her tanning bed–addicted friend buying celebrity mags and bottles of imported water.

Gothic Guy took his bag and left the store, lifting his sunglasses as soon as he stepped into the dusk.

The two women leered at him like they had just seen a walking zombie.

"That reminds me, Phyllis," the fitness queen whispered. "I saw that kid at Carlson's Book Store. He's so pale! Hasn't he ever heard of the sun? At least he could use some fake tanning cream. He needs a makeover bad!"

"Did you notice what he was reading?"

"Oh, yes," she recalled. "It was a book on Benson Hill Cemetery!"

"I'll have to tell Natalie Mitchell. She's convinced they're vampires!"

"Maybe we'll see the Sterlings in the tabloids next week: 'Vampire Teen Plays Baseball with Real Bats.'" And they giggled like me and Becky had before.

"Hurry!" I said, impatiently.

By the time Becky and I raced into the parking lot he was gone.

The gossip continued at our dinner table.

"John Garver at the courthouse told me that the Sterlings didn't buy the Mansion, but they inherited it," my dad said.

"Jimmy Fields said he heard they don't eat real food, but bugs and twigs," Nerd Boy added, like only a nerd would.

"What's the matter with you guys?" I shouted. "They're just different—they aren't breaking any laws!"

"I'm sure they aren't, Raven," my mom agreed. "But at the very least, they are strange. Their clothes are bizarre."

They all looked at me—at my black lipstick, black nail polish, blackened hair, black spandex dress, and clunky black plastic bracelets.

"Well, I dress bizarre, too. Do you think I'm strange?"

"Yes," they said in unison.

We all had a good laugh at that one, even me.

But deep down, I felt sad because I knew they really weren't kidding, and I could tell they felt sad, too, for the very same reason.

The sun had fallen from the sky and the moon was smiling over Becky and me. I was ready for the infiltration in camouflage night gear. I was wearing matte black lipstick instead of gloss, black turtleneck, black jeans, and a tiny black backpack with a flashlight and disposable camera. Mr. and Mrs. Sterling were in Europe. Their Mercedes was not in sight. Creepy Man must have gone to the store, and if he pushed his shopping cart as slowly as he drove, I'd have plenty of time.

The rusty iron gate stood in front of me. All the answers to the rumors lay on the other side. A quick climb over and the investigation would begin.

Unfortunately the adventure was going to be delayed, because Becky was terrified about climbing.

"You didn't tell me we'd have to climb the gate! I'm afraid of heights!"

"Please! Just get over. The clock is ticking."

Becky looked at the harmless old gate like it was Mt. Everest. "I can't. It's way too tall!"

"You can," I argued. "Here." I put my hands together for a boost. "You'll have to put your whole body weight into this!"

"I don't want to hurt you."

"You won't. Let's go."

"Are you sure?"

"Becky! I've waited months for this, and if you spoil it because you were afraid to step into my hand, I'll have to kill you."

She stepped and I grunted, and suddenly she was suctioned to the gate like a terrified spider.

"You can't just hang. You have to climb!"

She tried. She really did. I could see every muscle in her body strain. She wasn't heavy, but she wasn't strong either.

"Pretend you'll go to jail if you don't climb up."

"I'm trying!"

"Go, Becky, go!" I chanted like a cheerleader. She climbed slowly and finally reached the spiked top. Then she really freaked out.

"I can't go over. I'm scared."

"Don't look down."

"I can't move!"

I was starting to panic myself. She could have spoiled everything right then. A cop could have come by or some nosey neighbor. Or Gothic Guy himself might have come down from his attic to see what was making more noise than his blaring Cure CD.

"Here, I'll go." I pulled myself up the gate, maneuvered around Becky and flipped over the top. "Now you!" I whispered as I hung on the other side.

She didn't move. Her eyes weren't even open.

"I think I'm having a panic attack."

"Great!" I said, rolling my eyes. "You can't do this!" Maybe I should have brought Nerd Boy. "Becky?"

"I can't!"

"All right, all right! Slide down."

We both slithered down the iron gate on opposite sides. The iron bars separated us, but not our friendship.

"I hope I didn't spoil everything," Becky said.

"Hey, at least you gave me a ride."

She smiled appreciatively. "I'll keep an eye out here."

"No, go on home. Someone may see you."

"Are you sure?"

"It was fun hanging around with you," I joked. "But I gotta go now!"

"I hope you find everything you're looking for."

Becky drove off to the safety of her plaid couch and I continued on, minus one detective. I was the RBI—Raven Bureau of Investigation. I had to put an end to these rumors. And if they were more than just rumors, the world had to know.

The only light came from the curtained attic window. I could hear the faint wailing of an electric guitar, as I tiptoed around the side of the house. Fortunately, I didn't hear the sound of barking dogs. I found my favorite window. There were no boards or bricks, and the broken window had been replaced. If they fixed one thing in this Mansion, why did it have to be this particular window? I scrambled around and checked the other windows. They were all locked. Suddenly I noticed something catching the moonlight. I crouched over and lying by a bush was a hammer, and next to the hammer was the most beautiful thing I'd ever seen. It was a window, propped open with a brick. A caulking gun and putty were still sitting on the ledge. Someone had been working here and left their mess to dry. I kissed my new friend—the helpful brick—with my hand. Thank you, brick, thank you!

It was a much tighter squeeze through the window this time. I'd eaten a lot of candy since I was twelve.

I sucked in and pushed and pulled and grunted and heaved. I was through. I was in! I high-fived the air, the dark musty dusty basement air that filled the Mansion dungeon.

My flashlight guided me around crates and old furniture. I saw three rectangular objects leaning against the wall, covered with blankets. Paintings? My flesh tingled with anticipation as I grabbed the corner of the blanket and slowly pulled it back. I gasped. A face with two frozen eyes stared back at me. It was a mirror!

I clutched my racing heart. A covered mirror? I pulled the blankets off one after the other. They were all mirrors! Gold framed, wood framed, rectangular and oval. It couldn't be! Who covers their mirrors? Only vampires!

I continued to search the basement. I uncovered china dishes and crystal goblets, not the kind of glasses I was used to drinking from. Then I found a box that was labeled ALEXANDER'S WATERCOLORS, filled with drawings of an estate just like the one I was standing in.

There were other paintings, too: Spider-Man, Batman, and Superman. And a version of the big three together: Frankenstein, the Werewolf, and Count Dracula.

I started to put them into my backpack, but I had promised Becky I wouldn't take anything. So I took out my camera and took a photo instead.

I found a dusty rolled parchment with a faded family tree. There were long unpronounceable names of duchesses and barons going back centuries. And then at the bottom—Alexander. But no dates of births—or deaths!

Finally I uncovered three crates marked, SOIL. They had Romanian customs stamps on them.

As I made my way toward the stairs, I tripped over something covered with a white sheet. This was what I had come for—it had to be a coffin.

The object was the right size for a coffin and sounded like wood when I tapped my knuckles on it. I was as afraid as I was excited. I closed my eyes and yanked the sheet off. I took a deep breath and opened my eyes wide. It was only a coffee table.

I replaced the dusty sheet and carefully walked up the creaky stairs. I twisted the glass door handle and pushed, but to no avail. I pushed again with all my might, and the door suddenly burst open. I went flying into the hallway.

Portraits of a silver-haired man and woman lined the hallway, along with some wild paintings that could have been van Goghs or Picassos. I'd have known for sure if I had ever paid attention in art. I felt like I was in a museum, except there were candles and not fluorescent lights.

I tiptoed into the living room. The furniture was art deco. Very stylish. Huge red velvet curtains hung over the windows—the windows I had once waved a red baseball cap through. I could hear the Smiths pulsing through the ceiling.

I looked at my glow-in-the-dark Swatch. It was already eight-thirty. Time to leave. But I paused at the bottom of the grand staircase. I couldn't go upstairs. It would be ultra-risky. But I had to see everything. When would I ever get a chance like this again?

The first room I entered was a grand study, books upon books, the Sterlings' very own library. But no librarian, thank goodness. "Just came to check out *Crime and Punishment*" would not go over very well with Creepy Man. I peeked quickly into the other rooms. I had never seen so many bathrooms on one floor. Not even a football stadium had so many. A small guest bedroom was surprisingly spartan with a single bed. The master bedroom had a canopy bed with black lace curtains dripping around the columns. There was a vanity, but no mirror! Little combs and brushes and nail polishes. Shades of black, gray, and brown. I was about to look into the closet when the music suddenly stopped. I heard footsteps overhead.

I slipped down the stairs fast. I didn't look back and made sure not to lose my footing and stumble or fall like those girls do in *Friday the 13th* movies. Fiddling with the door locks, my fingers shook uncontrollably, like those foolish horror-flick girls. I was making way too much noise. As

I tried to unlock the top bolt, I saw the bottom bolt turning from the other side.

I ran down the hallway, but hearing footsteps coming from that direction, I doubled back and headed into the living room. There wasn't time to open the windows, so I threw myself behind the red velvet curtains.

"I'm back," I heard Creepy Man call in his thick Romanian accent. "Wexley's will be delivering tomorrow as usual. I'm going to retire now."

No one responded.

"You can't get them to shut up when they're three, but when they're seventeen they won't even open their mouths," I heard him mumbling to himself as he walked slowly past the grand staircase.

"Always leaving doors opened," I heard Creepy say and shut what must have been the door to the basement.

I peeled myself out of the curtain, ran, and unbolted all the front door locks in record time. I was ready to make my escape when I felt something familiar——a presence, again. I turned around and there he was standing in front of me. Gothic Guy. He stood motionless, like he was breathing in his uninvited guest.

When he extended his hand to me, to show I didn't have to be afraid, I noticed the accessory— he was wearing the black spider ring that I'd given Creepy Man on Halloween!

I had waited for a moment like this all my life. To see, to meet, to befriend someone who was different from everyone else, and just like me. Suddenly the reality of the situation hit me.

I had been caught.

I ran across the Mansion lawn and pumped and pulled and flung myself to the top of the rusty gate. And as I threw my booted foot over the top, I looked back and could see a distant figure standing in the doorway, watching me. I hesitated, feeling drawn back to the Mansion. I stared at him for a moment before sliding down to the other side.

I had found what I was looking for.

After calling Becky and describing my adventure in thrilling detail, I suffered from major insomnia. It wasn't nightfall keeping me awake, though; it was a guy with the deepest, darkest, dreamiest eyes that I had ever seen. My heart was spinning as much as my head. He was beautiful. His hair, his face, his lips. Absolutely amazing was the image of his extended hand—wearing my ring!

Why didn't he try to call the police? Why was he wearing my ring? Was he really a vampire? When would I see him again? I already missed Gothic Guy.

I was swinging high on the swing set the next morning at Evans Park, waiting for Becky, my head still dizzy from the previous night's encounter. I skidded to a stop when she finally arrived and I told her the whole incredible story again.

"You're lucky he didn't kill you!"

"Are you kidding? He was magnificent! I'd wait forever to meet someone half as cool!"

"So do you believe the rumors now?"

"I know it sounds crazy, but I think it could be true. There are so many signs. The drawing of Dracula, the candles, the sunglassses, the covered mirrors, the family tree."

"The mother's allergy to garlic and that the Sterlings have only been seen at night," Becky added.

"And what about the imported earth? Vampires always bring dirt from their native country."

"Are you going to call CNN?" she teased.

"Not yet. I need more proof."

"Would that involve trying to get me over that gate again?"

I began swinging, remembering Anne Rice, Bram Stoker, Bela Lugosi, *The Hunger*, *Lost Boys*, and all the Nosferatus that had ever graced the world with their wonderful smiles and slicked-back hair.

"No! It doesn't involve you at all," I finally answered her.

She let out a sigh of relief.

"There's really only one way to prove it, right? And then we can finally tell these gossip mongers to end their rumors for good. Then these Gothic angels can sleep peacefully, whether they go to bed during the night or day!" I joked.

"So what are you going to do, watch to see if he changes into a bat?"

"No. I'm going to watch to see if I do!"

"You can't change into a bat from watching him."

"I'll have to do more than look at him! There's only one way to tell if he's really a vampire."

"Yeah?"

"It'll be in his bite!" I screamed with excitement.

"You're going to have him bite you? Are you crazy?"

"Curiously crazy."

"But what happens if he is one? You'll turn into a vampire! Then what'll you do?"

"Then," I said, smiling, "I'll call CNN."

I sauntered home from Evans Park daydreaming about seeing my prince of darkness, when I spotted a black Mercedes turning the corner at the far end of my street.

I ran after it, as fast as I could, but combat boots can't compete with spinning wheels and motorized acceleration, even with Creepy driving.

At home I was greeted by a mischievously smiling Nerd Boy.

"I've got something for you!" he teased.

"Don't play games. I'm not in the mood."

"Seems as though the mail is now being delivered on Sundays. And the Sunday mailman is that weird butler from the Halloween Mansion!"

"What?"

"He delivered a letter for you!"

"Give it!"

"It'll cost you!"

"It'll cost you your head," I yelled, trying to jump on him.

He took off running and I followed in red-hot pursuit. "I'll get it. It's just a question of whether you're dead or alive when I do!"

If only I'd stayed home, Creepy Man would have given me the letter instead of Nerd Boy. Good thing my parents were out at lunch. They would have freaked if they'd seen a million-year-old man coming to the door and asking for me.

Nerd Boy waved the red envelope in front of my face, taunting me at every turn. Suddenly he ran upstairs. I grabbed his leg from behind and he fell. I pulled him toward me, but the envelope was in his outstretched arm, too far for me to grab.

I made a sharklike face to let him know I would bite his leg off if I had to, something you can do to a sibling and not go to jail. Panic set in, and he used his free foot to push my hands loose from his bony leg. He slammed his bedroom door in my face and turned the lock.

I banged and banged. My hands hurt but I wouldn't feel the throbbing till later, I was so mad.

"'Dear Raven,'" he pretended to read through the door. "'I love you and want you to be my witchy wife so we can have scary butler babies. Love, Weirdo Butler.'"

"Give that to me! Now! Don't you know what I'm capable of? Just ask the soccer team. I can make life a living hell for you!"

"I'll give it back on one condition."

"How much?"

"I don't want money."

"Then what?"

"That you promise . . ."

"What, already?"

"That you promise to stop calling me 'Nerd Boy'!"

There was silence on both sides of the door.

I felt a pang in my heart. Guilt? Pathos? I guess I never realized that my little nickname could have been hurting him so much all these years. That I had already made his life a living hell.

"Then what should I call you?"

"How about my name?"

"What would that be?" I teased.

"Billy."

"Uh, well . . . okay. You give me the letter, and I won't call you Nerd Boy—for a year."

"Forever."

"Forever?"

"Forever!"

"Okay. For . . . ever."

He cracked the door open and slipped the envelope out. He peered at me with his deep-brown baby-brother eyes.

"Here. I didn't open it."

"Thanks. You shouldn't have made me chase you. I've had a long day!"

"It's only twelve o'clock!"

"Exactly!" Now I had the red envelope safely in my hands. "Thanks, Nerd Boy." I couldn't help it. It was habit.

"You promised!". he yelled, slamming the door.

I knocked again. This time I felt the pain from the previous banging.

"What, Witch Girl?" he yelled. "Anyone would be a nerd compared to you! Leave me alone and go back to your cave!"

I found the door unlocked and stepped inside. It had been years since I'd been in his room. There were pictures of Michael Jordan and Wayne Gretzky on the wall and fifty billion computer games stacked on his floor and desk beside his computer. Nerd Boy was actually pretty interesting.

"Thanks for the letter," I said.

He just sat mousing at his computer, ignoring me.

"Billy!" I shouted. He quickly looked up, with shocked eyes. "I said, 'Thanks.' But I can't hug you. We'll save that for TV."

I threw myself on my bed, my black down comforter soft against my arms, and stared at the blank red envelope. It could say anything inside like: "Stay off our property or we'll sue you and your parents."

But at least I had the threat safely in my hands.

I gently opened the envelope, fearing the worst.

It was an invitation! "Mr. Alexander Sterling requests the company of Ms. Raven Madison at his home December 1 at 8:00 P.M. for dinner."

How did he know my name? How did he know where I lived? And was this real? No seventeen-year-old guy in this town, state, or country invited girls over like this. It was straight out of some Merchant-Ivory–Emma Thompson movie where people have stuffy British accents and are sandwiched into corsets and never say the word "love." It was so medieval, old-fashioned, out of this world. It was so romantic my flesh tingled all over.

I looked at the envelope for any other message, but that's all there was. It didn't even say "R.S.V.P." What nerve! He expected I would come, and he was right. I had waited for this all my life.

I couldn't tell my mother about my mysterious invitation to the Mansion. She'd say no, I couldn't go. I'd say yes, I could. She'd ground me; I'd run away. It would all be very dramatic. I was certain nothing could stop me from going, until my dad dropped a bomb on the morning of December 1.

"I'm taking Mom to Vegas tonight!" he said, pulling me aside. "It's all very spur-of-the-moment. We're flying out this afternoon."

"Isn't that romantic?" My mom beamed, grabbing a suitcase from the hall closet. "Your father's never done anything like this for our anniversary!"

"So you'll be in charge of the house and watching Billy," my dad ordered.

"Watch Billy? He's eleven!" I yelled, following them into their bedroom.

"Here's where we can be reached if you have any problems," he said, handing me a slip of paper with a phone number. "Your employment at Janice's proved to me you can be responsible. We'll be back tomorrow after dinner."

"But I have plans!"

"So invite Becky over here tonight." He tossed a hairbrush into his travel bag. "You're always going to her house. But pick out a movie you all can enjoy."

"Becky? That's the only friend you think I have? Like all I do with my life is watch TV?"

"Paul, should I take this?" my mom interrupted, holding a red strapless dress.

"I'm sixteen, Dad. I want to go out on a Saturday night!"

"I know," my mom said, placing a pair of red stilettos in her bag. "But not tonight. Your father's just surprised me! He hasn't done that since college. Just this once, Raven, then you can have all the Saturdays you want." She kissed me on the head, not waiting for a response.

"I'll be calling in at midnight sharp," my father warned, "just to make sure you and Billy are getting along and that my tennis racket is still in the closet."

"Don't worry. I'm not going to throw a wild party," I said angrily.

"Good, I might have to use the house as collateral at the blackjack table."

He went into his closet and pulled a jacket out. I went into my room and pulled my hair out. In all the seventeen years my parents had been married, my dad had to pick tonight to surprise my mom?

It was seven-thirty that night when I broke the news to Nerd Boy—rather, Billy Boy. I was wearing my Saturday-night best: a black spandex sleeveless mini-dress with a black lacy undertop that peeked through, black tights, unscuffed combat boots, black lipstick, and silver-and-onyx earrings.

"I'm going out tonight."

"But you're supposed to stay here." He ogled

my outfit like a protective father. "You have a date!"

"I do not. I just have to go."

"You can't! I won't let you. I'll tell." Billy Boy would have loved to stay by himself, but he loved his sudden power over me more.

"Becky's coming over to hang with you. You like Becky."

"Yeah, but does she like me?"

"She loves you!"

"Really?" he asked, with crush-boy eyes.

"I'll ask her when she gets here. Becky, do you love my little eleven-year-old brother?"

"Don't! You better not!"

"Then promise to behave."

"I'm going to tell. You're leaving me! Anything can happen. I could be on the internet and meet some crazy psycho woman that wants to marry me."

"You could only be so lucky," I said, looking out the window for Becky.

"You'll get in so much trouble!"

"Quit being a baby! Show Becky your computer games. She'll go mad over that alien spaceship stuff."

"If you leave, I'll call them in Vegas."

"Not if you value your life. I'll tie you to that chair if I have to!"

"Then do it, 'cause I'm going to call!" He ran for the cordless phone.

"Billy, please," I begged. "I really need to go. Someday you'll understand. Please, Billy."

He paused with the phone in his hand. He had never heard me beg him for anything, only threaten.

"Well, okay, just make sure you'll be here by midnight. I'm not going to pretend you're in the bathroom."

For the first time I can remember, I gave my brother a hug. And I gave him a real hug, a Ruby squeeze-hug, the kind that lets you really feel the other person's warmth.

"Where's Becky already!" he yelled, now playing for my team. "You need to leave!"

Suddenly the doorbell rang and we both flew down the steps. "Where were you?" I asked.

Becky sauntered in with a box of microwave popcorn. "I thought you said eight."

"I have to be there at eight!"

"Shoot, and I thought I was early. Take the

truck," she said, handing me her keys.

"Thanks. How do I look?" I asked, modeling my outfit.

"Wicked!"

"Really? Thanks!"

"You look like an angel of the night," my baby brother added.

I glanced in the hallway mirror and smiled. It might be the last time I would actually be able to see my reflection.

"Have fun, you two, and take good care of Billy, okay?"

"Who?" she asked, puzzled.

"Billy. My brother."

They both laughed. I grabbed my jacket and flew out of there like a bat.

Some hideous Dullsvillians had spray-painted GO HOME FREAKS! on the crumbling brick wall by the Mansion gate. It could have been Trevor. It could have been anyone. I felt an emptiness in my stomach.

I guess the Sterlings didn't get many visitors—there was no buzzer on the gate. Was I supposed to wait there, or climb over? But then I realized the gate was open. For me. I walked up the long driveway, looking at the curtained attic window, hoping I would be able to finally see it from the inside.

Anything could happen tonight. I really didn't know what to expect. What would we be eating for dinner? What do vampires eat anyway?

I gently rapped the serpent knocker.

The huge door slowly opened and Creepy Man greeted me with his crackly smile.

"So glad you could come," he said in his thick European accent, straight out of a black-and-white horror flick. "May I take your coat?"

He took my leather jacket somewhere.

I stood in the hallway, peering for signs of anything that seemed threatening. Where was my dinner partner anyway?

"Alexander will be joining you in a few minutes," Creepy said, returning. "Would you like to sit in the drawing room until he comes down?"

"Sure," I agreed, and was led to a huge room next to the living room. It was decorated simply with two scarlet Victorian chairs and a chaise longue. The only thing that didn't look dusty and old was the baby grand piano in the corner.

Creepy Man left again and I took the opportunity to snoop around. There were leather-bound books in some foreign language, dusty music scores, and old crinkly maps, and this wasn't even their library.

I caressed the smooth oak desk. What secrets lay inside its drawers? Then I felt that same unseen presence I had felt the last time I visited the Mansion. Alexander had come into the room.

He stood, mysteriously handsome. His hair was sleek and he wore a silk black shirt hanging over black jeans. I was anxious to see if he was wearing the spider ring, but he held his hands behind his back.

"I'm sorry I'm late. I was waiting for the baby-sitter," I confessed.

"You have a baby?"

"No, a brother!"

"Right," he said with an awkward laugh, his pale face coming to life. He was even more handsome than Trevor but didn't come off as self-assured, more like a wounded bird that needed to be held. As if he'd been living in a dungeon all his life and this was the first time he'd seen another human. He seemed uncomfortable with conversation and chose his words carefully, as if once spoken he might never get them back.

"I'm sorry I kept you waiting," he began. "I was getting you these." And he timidly held out five wildflowers.

Flowers? No way!

"Those are for me?" I was completely overwhelmed. It was like everything moved in slow motion. I took the flowers from him, softly touching his hands in the process. The spider ring caught my eye.

"I've never gotten flowers before. They're the most beautiful flowers I've ever seen."

"You must have a hundred boyfriends," he said, glancing down at his boots. "I can't believe they've never given you flowers."

"When I turned thirteen my grandmother sent me a bouquet of tulips in a plastic yellow pot." As dumb as it sounded, it was better than saying, "I've never gotten flowers from my hundred boyfriends, because I've never had one boyfriend!"

"Flowers from grandmothers are very special," he replied strangely.

"But why five?"

"One for every time I saw you."

"I had nothing to do with the spray paint—"

Creepy Man appeared. "Dinner is ready. Shall I put those in some water, miss?"

"Please," I said, though I didn't want to part with them.

"Thank you, Jameson," Alexander said.

Alexander waited for me to exit the room first, straight out of a Cary Grant movie, but I was unsure which way to go.

"I thought you'd know the way," he teased. "Would you like something to drink?"

"Sure, anything." Wait a minute—anything? So I said, "Actually, water will be great!"

He returned a moment later with two crystal goblets. "I hope you're hungry."

"I'm always hungry," I flirted. "And you?"

"Rarely hungry," he said. "But always thirsty!"

He led me into the candlelit dining room, dominated by a long uncovered oak table set with ceramic plates and silver utensils. He pulled out my chair, then sat a million miles away at the other end of the table. The five wildflowers stood in a crystal vase blocking my view.

Creepy Man—I mean, Jameson—wheeled in a creaky cart and presented me with a basket of steamy rolls. He returned with crystal bowls filled with a greenish soup. Considering the number of courses, the slowness of Jameson's service and the length of the table, we were guaranteed to be here for months. But I didn't care, I didn't want to be anywhere else in the world.

"It's Hungarian goulash," Alexander stated as I nervously stirred the pasty soup. I had no idea what—or who—was in it, and as Alexander and Jameson waited for my reaction, I realized I'd have to taste it.

"Yum!" I exclaimed, slurping down half a spoonful. It was way more delicious than any soup I'd ever eaten from a can, but one hundred times as spicy!

My tongue was on fire and I immediately chugged down my water.

"I hope it's not too spicy," Alexander said.

"Spicy?" I gasped, my eyes bursting. "You've got to be joking!"

Alexander motioned for Jameson to bring more water. It seemed like an eternity, but he returned with a pitcher. Eventually I got my breath back. I didn't know what to ask Alexander, but I wanted to know everything about him.

I could tell Alexander had fewer friends than I. He seemed uncomfortable in his own skin.

"What do you do all day?" I inquired like a TV reporter breaking the ice.

"I wanted to know the same thing about you," he offered.

"I go to school. What do you do?"

"Sleep."

"You sleep?" This was major news! "Really?" I asked skeptically.

"Is there something wrong with that?" he said, awkwardly brushing his hair from his eyes.

"Well, most people sleep at night."

"I'm not most people."

"True . . ."

"And you're not either," he said, staring at me with his soulful eyes. "I could tell when I saw you on Halloween dressed as a tennis player. You seemed a little too old to trick-or-treat. And you had to be different to think that was a costume."

"How did you get my info?"

"Jameson was supposed to return the tennis racket to you but gave it to a blond soccer player who said he was your boyfriend. I might have bought the story if I hadn't seen you smack his hand and drive off without him."

"Well, you're right, he's not my boyfriend. He's a totally lamoid jerk at school."

"But fortunately he also told Jameson your name and address to back up his story. That's how I knew how to find you. I didn't think I'd find you exploring the house again."

His dreamy eyes stared right through me.

"Well . . . I . . ."

Our laughter echoed in the Mansion.

"Where are your parents?" I asked.

"Romania."

"Romania? Isn't Romania where Dracula lived?" I inquired, hinting.

"Yes."

My eyes lit up. "Are you related to Dracula?" I asked.

"He never came to a family reunion," he teased in an anxious voice. "You're a wacky girl. You certainly give life to Dullsville."

"Dullsville? No way! That's what I call this town!"

"Well, what else could we call it? There isn't

any nightlife here, is there? Not for people like me and you."

Nightlife. People like me and you. You mean vampires, I wanted to say.

"I preferred living in New York and London," he went on.

"I bet there's a lot to do there at night. And a lot of night people." Just then Jameson came to take the goulash away and served us steak.

"I hope you're not a vegetarian," he said.

I peered down at my dinner. The steak was medium rare, more on the rare side, as the juice spilled onto the plate and into the mashed potatoes.

He was so mysterious, and funnier than I could have imagined. I was under his spell as I peered at him through the flowers.

"I'm sure it'll be delicious," I said. He watched as I took a bite. "Yum, once again."

Suddenly he looked at me with sad eyes. "Listen, do you mind—"

He picked up his plate and walked over to me. "All I can see are the wildflowers, and after all, you're much prettier."

He set his plate next to mine and dragged his

oak chair over. I thought I would faint. He sat smiling as we ate, his leg softly touching mine. My body was electrified. Alexander was funny, gorgeous, and awkward in a sexy way. I wanted to know his whole life story. No matter how many years he had lived, seventeen or seventeen hundred.

"What do you do at night? Where else have you lived? Why don't you go to school?" I rattled on suddenly.

"Slow down."

"Um . . . where were you born?"

"Romania."

"Then where's your Romanian accent?"

"In Romania. We traveled constantly."

"Have you ever gone to school?"

"No, I've always had a private tutor."

"What's your favorite color?"

"Black."

I remembered Mrs. Peevish. I paused and asked, "What do you want to be when you grow up?"

"You mean I'm not grown up?"

"That's a question, not an answer," I said coyly.

"What do you want to be?" he asked.

I stared into his deep, dark mysterious eyes and whispered, "A vampire."

He stared at me curiously and seemed disturbed. And then he laughed. "You are a riot!" Then he looked at me sharply. "Raven, why did you sneak into the house?"

I looked away, embarrassed.

Jameson wheeled over some pastry on a cart. He lit a match and flames rose around the dessert. "Flambé!" he announced. And just in time.

Alexander extinguished our desserts and told Jameson we would finish our dinner outside. "I hope you aren't afraid of the dark," he said, leading me into the dilapidated gazebo.

"Afraid? I live for it!"

"Me, too," he said, smiling. "It's really the only way to see the stars properly." He lit a half-melted candle on the ledge.

"Do you bring all your girlfriends here?" I asked, fingering the used candle.

"Yes." He laughed. "And I read to them by candlelight. What would you like?" he asked, pointing to a stack of textbooks on the floor. "*Functions and Logarithms* or *Minority Group Cultures?*"

I laughed.

"The moon is so beautiful tonight," he said, staring out the gazebo.

"Makes me think of werewolves. Do you think a man can change into an animal?"

"If he's with the right girl," he said with a laugh.

I moved closer to him. The moonlight softly lit his face. He was beautiful. *Kiss me, Alexander. Kiss me now!* I thought, closing my eyes.

"But we have all of eternity," he suddenly said. "For now let's enjoy the stars."

He placed his dessert bowl on the ledge and blew out the candle, and I quickly grabbed his hand. It wasn't a Trevor hand or a skinny Billy Boy hand. He had the best hand in the whole world!

We lay down on the cold grass and gazed up at the stars, holding hands.

We relaxed in silence, our hands warming together. I could feel the prickly legs of the spider ring.

I wanted to kiss. But he just stared up at the stars.

"Who are your friends?" I asked, turning to him.

"I keep to myself."

"I bet you met tons of cool girls before you moved here."

"Cool is one thing. The kind of girls who accept you for who you really are is another. I'd like something . . . lasting."

Lasting? For eternity? But I couldn't ask that.

"I want a relationship I can finally sink my teeth into."

Really? Well, I'm your girl! I thought. But he didn't turn toward me; instead, Alexander gazed at the sky.

"So you don't have *any* friends here?" I asked, trying to pump him for more info.

"Just one."

"Jameson?"

"Someone who wears black lipstick."

We both stared up at the moon in silence. I beamed from his compliment.

"Who do you hang out with?" he finally asked.

"Becky is the only one who accepts me, and

it's because I'm the only one who doesn't beat her up." We both laughed. "Everyone else thinks I'm weird."

"I don't."

"Really?" No one had ever said that to me in my whole life. No one.

"You seem a lot like me," he said. "You don't gawk at me like I'm a freak."

"I'll kick anyone who does."

"I think you already did. Or at least smacked him with a racket."

We laughed in the moonlight, and I placed my free arm on his chest and hugged him, as my Gothic Mate softly stroked my arm.

"Could those be ravens?" I asked, pointing to a flurry of dark wings circling high above the Mansion.

"Those aren't birds—they're bats."

"Bats! I've never seen bats around here, until you moved in."

"Yeah, we found some hanging in the attic. Jameson set them free. I hope they don't frighten you. They're wonderful creatures."

"It takes one to know one, right?" I hinted.

"But don't worry. They never swoop down and get tangled in jet-black hair like yours. Only in mall hair."

"They like hairspray?"

"They hate it. They know mall hair looks terrible!"

I laughed, and he began softly stroking my hair. His touch calmed me. I thought I was going to melt into the earth.

He was certainly taking much more time than Trevor had. I began stroking his hair, which was silky from his gel.

"Do bats like gel?" I asked.

"They love the way it looks with a silk Armani," he teased back.

I wriggled over him and pinned his arms down. He looked up at me with surprise and smiled. I waited for him to kiss me. But he didn't move. Of course, he didn't move—I was pinning him down! What was I thinking?

"Tell me your favorite thing about bats, Bat Girl," he asked, as I anxiously stared down at him.

"They can fly."

"You want to fly?"

I nodded.

He wrestled me over and pinned my arms down. Again I waited for him to kiss me, but he didn't. He just stared into my eyes.

"So what's your favorite thing about bats, Bat Boy?" I asked.

"I'd have to say," he began, thinking, "their vampire teeth."

I gasped, but it wasn't because of Alexander's comment. A mosquito had bitten my neck.

"Don't be afraid," he said, squeezing my hand. "I won't bite . . . yet." He laughed at his joke.

"I'm not afraid. A mosquito bit me!" I explained, scratching like mad.

He examined the mark like a doctor. "It's starting to swell. We'd better get you ice."

"It'll be okay. I get these all the time."

"I don't want you to tell your parents you came over to my house and got bitten!"

I wanted to tell the whole world I was bitten, but that mosquito had ruined everything.

He took me into the kitchen and put ice on my tiny wound. I listened to the grandfather clock chime away. Nine . . . *Chime* . . . Ten . . .

Chime. No! Eleven . . . *Chime.* Frig! Twelve. It couldn't be!

"I've got to go!" I exclaimed.

"So soon?" he asked, disappointed.

"Any second my dad will be calling from Vegas, and if I'm not there to answer, I'll be grounded for eternity!"

If only I could stay and live with Alexander in his attic room and have Creepy Man serve me Count Chocula cereal every morning . . .

"Thanks for the flowers and the dinner and the stars," I said hurriedly by Becky's truck, scrambling in my purse for the keys.

"Thank you for coming."

He looked dreamy and gorgeous, and somehow lonely. I wanted my Gothic Vampire Mate to kiss me now. I wanted his mouth on my neck and his soul within mine.

"Raven?" he said cautiously.

"Yes?"

"Would you like me to . . ."

"Yes? Yes?"

"Would you like me to . . . invite you again, or would you rather sneak back in?"

"I'd love to be invited," I answered, waiting. If

he kissed me now, we'd be bonded for all eternity.

"Wonderful then. I'll call you." He kissed me softly on the cheek. The cheek? Still, it was softer and more romantic than the time Jack Patterson had kissed me outside the Mansion, and much more romantic than Trevor pushing me against a tree. And as much as I wanted a real kiss—a vampire kiss—he was changing me. I was transforming into a swooning noodle-legged, goopy, googly-eyed, drippy marshmallow girl.

I could still feel his lovely, full lips against my face as I drove home. My body tingled all over with excitement, longing, passion—feelings I had never felt about a guy before. And as I scratched the bite that wasn't his, I could only hope I wouldn't turn into a blood-sucking mosquito.

"Dad's explaining to Becky the rules of blackjack," Billy whispered anxiously, as I ran through the door. "He's already told her about every casino and the history of Siegfried and Roy. He's running out of hotels on the strip!"

I whispered, "Thanks," to Becky and quickly grabbed the phone.

"Becky loves to talk," my dad began. "I had

no idea she was so fascinated with Las Vegas. Next time I'll bring her. She tells me you guys have been watching vampire movies all evening."

"Yeah . . ."

"*Revenge of Dracula* for the fiftieth time?"

"No. It's a new one. It's called *Vampire Kisses*."

"Is it good?"

"I give it two thumbs up!"

B ecky and I were eating ice-cream cones—
Vanilla Royale and Chocolate Attack—outside Shirley's Bakery the next day.

"Alexander's the dreamiest! I can still feel his
lips tingling against my cheek," I said. "Becky, for
the first time I don't want to run away from this
town, 'cause at the top of Benson Hill lives my
Gothic dream guy. I can't stop thinking about
him. I only wish you'd met him, too, then you'd
know how spectacular he is!"

Suddenly a red Camaro pulled up.

"Matt saw Becky's truck parked outside

Freaky Mansion last night," Trevor proclaimed in his ornery way as he sauntered over. He stared into Becky's face and asked, "Trying to spray paint the Mansion, Igor?"

"No," I defended, smiling, still thinking about last night. I wasn't going to let Trevor spoil my wonderful mood.

"So you weren't up to trouble, Werewolf Girl?" Trevor asked, continuing to stare at Becky.

Becky looked scared.

"Let's go, Trev," Matt said.

"We'd love to chat with you lovely gentlemen, but we're in the middle of a corporate meeting," I told him. "So you'll have to leave a message with my secretary."

"Is Shirley putting Prozac in her ice cream now?" Trevor said, laughing. "I don't think you'd know what a gentleman was if he bit you on the neck!"

I continued to lick the edge of my cone.

"Or was it you up there?" Trevor guessed. "You're always up to trouble."

"Maybe it was Becky's parents; it's their truck. It doesn't take a rocket scientist to figure that one out."

"I just thought that maybe you and Becky were dating the Osbournes! Oh, I forgot, he just bites the heads off bats—he doesn't turn into them."

"I think I hear your mother calling," I said.

"They're just like you, you know, miserably pale, and social outcasts. They haven't even tried to join the country club yet. But then again we don't accept vampires."

"Vampires?" I laughed uneasily. "Who says that?"

"Everyone, pinhead! The Sterling vampires. The dude hangs out in the cemetery. But I think they're just escaped lunatics like you. They're total freaks."

"C'mon, Trev, let's get out of here already. We've got practice," Matt said.

"Now I see who wears the pants in your relationship," I said. "But I forgot, your pants wound up on my locker."

Trevor grabbed the cone from my hand.

"Hey, give it back!" I shouted. Trevor had managed to spoil my blissful mood after all.

He took a huge lick.

"Great, now it has disgusting snob germs.

You can keep it," I said.

"Baby, it had germs the moment you looked at it."

"Let's go, Becky," I said, tugging her arm.

"Leaving so soon?"

"I thought I was done with you!" I shouted.

"Done? You're always trying to break my heart, aren't you? Does this mean our engagement is off?"

"Let's go, Trev," Matt said. "We've got things to do."

"You know you love this, Monster Girl. If it wasn't for me, no one would pay attention to you."

"And I'd be the luckiest girl in the world."

"I'll see you in the car," Matt impatiently told Trevor.

"I'll be right there," Trevor replied, then leaned into me. "If you want to be the luckiest girl in the world, you'll go with me to the Snow Ball."

Trevor was asking me to a dance? And of all dances, the Snow Ball? The big school dance where plastic icicles and snowflakes hung from the gym rafters, and fake snow covered the gym floor? He'd show up with me on his arm in front of all his friends? The soccer snobs and the hundred-dollar-haircut girls? It had to be a big joke. I'd be gussied up, waiting at my house, and he'd stand me up, or he'd dump a bucket of red goo on me like in *Carrie*. But even if he was serious, even if by some miracle Trevor really did like me, I couldn't go to the ball with him. Not now that I had met Alexander Sterling.

"It'll be a night you'll never forget," he said seductively.

"I'm sure it will, but I don't want to have nightmares for the rest of my life."

"Just can't tear yourself away from Nick at Nite."

"No. I'm already going."

Trevor sneered. "Stag? Or with an inflatable doll?"

"I have a date."

Becky gasped, but she and Trevor weren't the only ones surprised by my rash words.

"In your dreams! I was only asking you out of pity. No one else would show up with you, unless he was dead."

"Well, we'll just see about that, won't we?"

"I'm leaving," Matt shouted from the car.

"Are you coming?"

"Thanks for the ice cream, psycho," Trevor said, getting into the Camaro. "But next time remember, I prefer Rocky Road."

I watched my double-dip Chocolate Attack screech away.

"I'd offer you mine, but I know you don't like pure vanilla," Becky said consolingly.

"Thanks, but I have bigger things than ice cream to worry about. Like getting a date!"

Every time the phone rang, my heart jumped. Was it Alexander? And when it wasn't him my heart would break into a million pieces. It had been two long days since I had seen my Gothic mate. I was so preoccupied with Alexander, dreaming of the next time we'd be together, nothing else mattered. I didn't wash the spot where his tender love lips had pressed against my flesh. I was acting like I was straight out of a Gidget movie! What had happened to me? I was losing my edge! For the first time in my life I was really afraid. Afraid of never seeing him again and afraid of being rejected.

If I asked Alexander to the dance, he might

freak out. He might say, "With you?" or "No way, not a lame, school dance. I'm so beyond that! And I thought you were, too."

I was beyond that, even though I'd never gone to any dances to actually get beyond them. I wouldn't be going to homecoming or the prom or any of the other dances scheduled throughout the school year. I would stay home with Becky and watch the *Munsters* on TV. But Trevor's challenge had forced me to fight back, with a weapon that I didn't even have: Alexander.

This feeling of not being able to eat or sleep was new to me. To hang my heart on every ring of the phone, to scream at the top of my lungs for Billy Boy not to tie up the line with his addictive web surfing, not to be able to watch *Nosferatu* without crying, or to listen to a silly, sappy, drippy, lovesick Celine Dion song without thinking she had written it just for me—I wanted it all to go away.

I think some people call this love. I called it hell.

And then it happened. After two long, torture-filled days. When the phone rang, I thought it was for Billy Boy, and when Billy Boy called my name, I thought it was Becky. I was ready to pour my heart out to her. But before I could speak, I heard his dreamy voice.

"I couldn't wait any longer," he said.

"Excuse me?" I asked, surprised.

"It's Alexander. I know guys aren't supposed to call right away. But I couldn't wait any longer."

"That's a stupid rule. I could have moved."

"In two days?"

"It was only two days?"

He laughed. "It seemed a year for me."

His comment was like a love letter sent straight to my heart.

I waited for him to go on, but there was silence. He said nothing more. This was the perfect chance to invite him to the Snow Ball. The worst he could do was hang up. My hands were shaking and my confidence was oozing out with my perspiration. "Alexander . . . um . . . I have something to ask you."

"I do, too."

"Well, you first."

"No, ladies first."

"No, guys are supposed to do the asking."

"You're right." There was silence. "Well . . . would you like to go out? Tomorrow night?"

I smiled with delight! "Go out? Yeah, that would be great!"

"So what were you going to ask me?"

I paused. I can do this! I took a deep breath. "Would you . . ."

"Yes?"

"Do you . . ."

"Do I what?"

"Like to dance?"

"Yeah, but I didn't think this town had any hip clubs. You know of one?"

"No . . . but when I find one, I'll let you know." I was such a wimpola!

"Great! Then I'll see you tomorrow at my house, after sundown."

"After sundown?"

"You said you lived for the darkness. So do I."

"You remembered."

"I remember everything," he said, and hung up the phone.

My first date! Becky said my first date was dinner at the Mansion, but I didn't agree. Tonight we would be going out: to watch a movie, to play miniature golf, to share a soda at Shirley's. I spent all afternoon talking with Becky, speculating about where he'd take me, what he'd be wearing, and when he would kiss me.

I was so excited, I ran the whole way there. I had to meet Alexander at his iron gate. My mom would have freaked if she had known I had a date with the guy who lived in a haunted house. I couldn't bear the thought of his showing up at my door and my dad's asking him questions about tennis players and his plans for college. So I had to meet my Romeo on his balcony.

And there he was, leaning against the iron gate, sexy in his black jeans and black leather jacket, holding a backpack.

"Are we going on a hike?" I asked.

"No, a picnic."

"At this hour?"

"Is there a better time?"

I shook my head, with a smile.

I had no idea where Alexander would take me, but I could imagine the response from our fellow Dullsvillians.

"Doesn't this bother you?" I asked, pointing to the graffiti.

Alexander shrugged. "Jameson wanted to paint over it, but I wouldn't let him. One man's graffiti is another man's masterpiece." He took my hand and led me down the street without any hints of our plans for the night. And I didn't care where we were going, just as long as it was a million miles away and he never let go.

We stopped at Dullsville's cemetery.

"Here we are," he said.

I had never been taken out on a date, much less a date to a cemetery. Dullsville's cemetery dated from the early 1800s. I'm sure Dullsville was much more exciting as a pioneer town—tiny dress shops, saloons, traders, gamblers, and those Victorian lace-up boots that were totally in.

"Do you bring all your dates here?" I asked.

"Are you afraid?" he asked.

"I used to play here as a child. But during the day."

"This cemetery is probably the most lively place in town."

The rumors were true. Alexander did come to the cemetery in the dark.

The creepy gate was locked to ensure uneasy access for Dullsville's vandals.

"We'll have to climb," he said. "But I know how you like climbing gates."

"We can get in trouble for this," I pointed out.

"But it's okay to sneak into houses, right?" he asked. "Don't worry. I know one of the people."

Dead? Alive? A corpse? Maybe a cousin of Jameson's worked the graveyard shift—literally.

Alexander turned away as I struggled to get

over in my tight spandex dress.

After we both dusted off, he took my hand and led me down the middle path, where gravestones were lined up for miles. Some of the grave markers signfied a plague that devastated in the 1800s. Alexander walked briskly like he knew exactly where he was going.

Where was he leading me? Who did he know here? Did he sleep here? Had he brought me here to kiss me? And would I become a vampire?

I slowed down. Did I really want to be a vampire? And call this my home? For all eternity?

I tripped over the handle of a shovel, which sent me tumbling forward. I started to fall into an empty grave. Alexander grabbed my arm in the nick of time.

I hung over the empty grave, staring down into the darkness.

"Don't be afraid. It doesn't have your name on it," Alexander joked.

"I think I'm supposed to be home," I said nervously, brushing graveyard dirt off my dress.

But he led me further into the cemetery with his strong hand.

Suddenly we were standing atop a small hill

beneath a giant marble monument.

He picked up some fresh daffodils that had blown away and replaced them tenderly at the foot of Baroness Sterling's monument.

"I'd like you to meet someone," he said, looking at me gently and then at the grave. "Grandma, this is Raven."

I didn't know what to say as I stared at the marker. I had never *met* a dead person before. What was I supposed to say—"She looks just like you"?

But of course, he didn't expect me to say anything as he sat down on the grass and drew me next to him.

"Grandma used to live here—I mean in town. She left us the house and we finally got it after years of probate. I always loved the Mansion."

"Wow. The baroness was your grand-mother?"

"I visit her when I feel lonely. She under-stood what it felt like to be alone. She didn't fit in with the Sterling side of the family. Grandpa died in the war. She said I always reminded her of him." He took a deep breath and looked up at the stars. "It's beautiful here, don't you think?" he went on. "There aren't many lights to block out the stars. It's like the universe is a huge canvas, with sprinkles of light that twinkle and glisten, like a painting that is always there, just waiting to be looked at. But people don't notice it because they're too busy. And it's the most beautiful work of all. Well, almost—"

We were silent for a few minutes, gazing at the heavens. I heard only his soft breath and the sound of crickets. All first dates should be as wonderful as this. It totally beat a first-run movie.

"So your grandma's the lady that stared out the wind—uh, I mean she, well . . ."

"She was a wonderful artist. She taught me how to paint superheroes and monsters. Lots of monsters!"

"I know."

"You know?"

"I mean, I know it must be hard for you. But I like vampires, too!" I hinted.

He seemed to be thinking of something else. "I traveled so much, and since I was home-schooled, I never had the chance to fit in any-where."

He looked so lost, so soulful, so lonely. I wanted him to kiss me now. I wanted to let him know I was his for all eternity.

"Let's eat," he suddenly said, climbing to his feet.

He placed five black candles in ornate votive holders and lit them with an antique lighter. He unpacked a bottle of sparkling juice and crackers and cheese and spread a black lace tablecloth over the cold grass.

"Have you ever been in love?" I asked as he filled my crystal goblet.

Suddenly we heard a howl and the candles blew out.

"What was that?" I asked.

"I think it's a dog."

"It sounds more like a wolf!"

"Either way, we'd better go!" he said urgently.

I started to shove everything into his backpack.

"We don't have time for that!" he said, grabbing my hand.

The wind continued to howl. The noise was getting closer.

We hid behind the monument.

"If it's a ghost you've come to see," a familiar

voice called to us, "I can assure you that the only ghost you'll be seeing tonight is your own."

A man followed with a flashlight. It was Old Jim, the caretaker, with Luke, his Great Dane.

If he recognized me here at this hour I'd have to bribe him with a year's supply of dog biscuits to keep him from telling my parents.

We peeked out and could see the dog licking juice off the grass.

"Give me that, Luke," Old Jim said and picked up the bottle. He took a long swig.

"Now!" Alexander whispered. He tightened his grip on my hand and we ran, scampering over the fence.

I don't think a real ghost and a phantom wolf could have scared me more than Old Jim and his rusty Luke.

"I guess I should have taken you to a movie after all," Alexander said with a smile after we caught our breath. "I'll walk you home."

"Can we go to your house?" I pleaded. "I want to see your room!"

"You can't see my room."

"We have time."

"No way."

There was an edginess in his voice I hadn't heard before.

"What's in your room, Alexander?"

"What's in your room, Raven?" he asked, glaring at me. "Let's go back to your place."

"Uh . . . well . . ." He was right. I couldn't bring him into my house and subject him to Billy Boy and my white-bread parents. Not on our first date. "My room's a mess."

"Well, mine is, too," he said.

"I don't have to go home, really."

"I don't want to get you in trouble."

"I always get in trouble. My mom wouldn't recognize me if I wasn't in trouble."

But the streets we walked, hand-in-hand, led back to my house, and no matter how slowly I walked, before I knew it we were standing on my doorstep, saying good-bye.

"Well . . . until . . . next time . . ." he said, his face shining beneath the porch light.

"Next time the mortuary?"

"I thought we could watch a movie at my house."

"You have a TV?" I said. "It's powered by electricity, you know."

"Sassy girl, I have Bela Lugosi's *Dracula* on DVD, since you like vampires so much."

"*Dracula*? Awesome!"

"Then it's a date. Seven o'clock tomorrow, okay?"

"Sensational!"

We had made another date and there was nothing to do now but say good-bye. Primo moment for a luscious kiss. He put his hand on my shoulder and leaned in, his eyes closed and his lips full.

Suddenly the door locks rattled. Alexander stepped out of the light and into the bushes.

"I thought I heard voices," my mom said, opening the door. "Where's Becky?"

"She's at home." It was actually the truth.

"I don't like you running off without telling me," she scolded, holding the door open for me.

Longing to have that moment back and one moment more, I looked over at Alexander.

"Did you guys go to the movies?" she asked as I reluctantly stepped inside.

"No, Mom, we went to the cemetery."

"For once, I wish you would give me a straight answer!"

For once, I was giving her a straight answer.

And as I looked over my shoulder for a final glimpse of my Gothic Dream Mate, she closed the door on my heavenly first date.

I was always late for everything—dinner, school, even movies—but tonight I was early, as I arrived at the Mansion at 6:45. Alexander opened the door himself and kissed me politely on the cheek. I was as shocked as he at his sudden display of affection.

"That never happened when Jameson opened the door!" I said.

"Well, you better tell me if it does. We have a rule, you know. I don't kiss his girls and he doesn't kiss mine!" Alexander glowed even more than he had that night I'd snuck in and he had extended the hand with the spider ring. He was growing confident.

He led me up the grand staircase to the family room. It was filled with modern art pieces—flowered paintings, an Andy Warhol print of Campbell's soup cans, Barbie doll sculptures, and flashy, furry, wild rugs. There was a black leather couch, a big-screen TV, and a glass table with a giant tub of movie popcorn, SnoCaps, Dots, Sprees, Good & Plenty, and two neon-green glasses filled with pop.

"I wanted to make you feel like you're at the movies," he explained.

He put in the DVD and turned out the lights, and we snuggled together in the darkness. I picked SnoCaps and he chose a pack of Sprees. The popcorn rested between us on the couch.

Dracula was getting ready to take a bite out of Lucy when Alexander gently pulled my face away from the screen.

He stared me at with his deep midnight eyes. He leaned toward me. And he kissed me. With passion. He kissed me! He finally kissed me! Right there in front of Bela Lugosi!

He kissed me as if he were drinking me in

and filling my heart and veins with love. As I took a breath, he began kissing my ears and gently nibbling them. I giggled like crazy. His lips and teeth made their way down my neck, his mouth filling me with total passion. His soft biting on my neck tickled. I was so into his spell, I stretched my legs out clumsily on the coffee table, spilling Alexander's glass and then the popcorn over him. Alexander, startled, sunk his teeth into my neck so hard I screamed.

"Oh, no! I'm sorry!" he apologized.

Popcorn was scattered everywhere and I held my neck, which was pulsing like my heart.

"Raven, are you okay?"

The blood rushed from my brain, and the room began to turn one way then another, and my stomach felt nauseated. I did what any overexcited, sappy girl would do. I fainted dead away.

It seemed like hours later, but it was only seconds. I awoke to Alexander calling my name. Dracula was still in Lucy's room. The only difference was the lights were on.

"Raven? Raven?"

"What happened?"

"You fainted! I thought that only happened

in old movies!"

"Here, drink this." He put my glass to my lips, like I was a baby.

Alexander's pale face was even paler. He took some ice that had spilled on the table and placed it on my neck. "I'm so sorry! I never meant to—"

"That's cold!" I cried.

"I've ruined everything," he said, holding the dripping ice on my neck.

"Don't say that. This happens all the time."

He looked at me skeptically.

"Well, just with you."

"I never meant to hurt you."

I could feel his fingers tracing the wound. "It's just a flesh wound. I didn't break the skin."

"You didn't?" I asked, almost disappointed.

"This is bigger than the mosquito bite. You'll have one major hickey!"

"Bela would be proud," I said, hanging on Alexander's reaction.

"Yes," he said. "I guess he would."

"I want to ask you something," I said nervously, as he walked me to my door. I was running out of chances to invite him to the dance, and I realized if I didn't ask him now, I never would.

"You don't want to hang out anymore? Listen, Raven—"

"No, I mean . . . I just wanted to say . . ."

"Yes?"

"Umm . . . I found a place to dance," I began.

"To dance? In this town?"

"Yes."

"Is it cool?"

"No, but—"

"But if you go there, it must be the trendiest place in the world."

"It's my school."

"School?"

"I thought you would think it was totally lame. I shouldn't have mentioned it."

"I've never been to a school dance before."

"Really? Me neither."

"Then it'll be the first time for both of us," he said with a sexy and suddenly confident grin.

"I guess it will. It's called the Snow Ball. I can wear a woolen scarf to cover my bite," I joked.

"I'm sorry—it was an accident."

"It was the best accident that ever happened to me!"

He leaned in to kiss me and stopped suddenly. "I better not."

"You better!"

He leaned in again, and this time our lips melted together, his strong hand gently holding my chin.

"Until we meet again," he said, kissing me one last time. He blew me a final kiss when he reached the car.

I touched the mark where he had bitten me. I knew I was already changing. But I wanted to look in the mirror to see for sure.

The following day Becky and I went to Evans Park immediately after school. We opened our backpacks in a darkened corner of the empty rec center. My camera, my journal, and a compact mirror lay before us. Finally Becky placed a Tupperware bowl that held a clove of garlic and a cross wrapped in a leather pouch on the floor.

"Ready to see the bite?" I asked.

"Is it gross?"

"It's my love wound," I said and carefully unwrapped the black scarf I'd been wearing all day.

"Wow! He has a big mouth!" she said, wide-eyed.

"Isn't it cool?"

"I can see teeth marks. A few scrapes, but I don't think he punctured the skin. Does it hurt?"

"Not at all. It's like getting your ears pierced—it stings at first, but the pain quickly goes away."

"Did you faint when you got your ears pierced, too?"

"Don't get smart!"

"And the mark will go away, too, won't it?"

"That's what we're here to find out. Get the camera."

Becky took pictures of my wound, front and side. We laid the Polaroids on the cement floor as they developed.

"You're showing up," Becky stated.

"Okay. Now the mirror," I said.

"Are you sure?"

"Yes."

"But if you are—you know, if you're really a . . . this could hurt."

"Becky, we don't have all day."

I took off my sunglasses.

"Ready?" she asked, holding the compact.

"Ready."

She opened the compact and pushed it against my nose.

"Ouch!"

"Oh, no!"

"You're not supposed to hit me with it! Give that to me!" I grabbed the compact with trembling hands and stared hard. Nothing—or rather, everything. I was still reflecting.

"Try the garlic!" I ordered, tossing the mirror aside.

Becky opened the Tupperware bowl and cut the clove in half.

"Now?" she asked.

"Now."

I could smell the garlic already. She held the clove under my nose. I took a deep whiff. And coughed wildly.

"Are you okay?"

"Man, that's strong! Gross! Put it away!"

"It's fresh—that's why."

"Put it away!" I said.

"I like the smell. It clears my sinuses."

"Well, it's not supposed to relieve me of

nasal congestion. It's supposed to send me into a revolting frenzy."

"We have one more shot left."

She opened the leather pouch. "Ready?"

I took a deep breath. "Go for it!"

She pulled out a jeweled cross on a gold chain.

"Wow, that's cool," I said. "It looks very special."

"Does it bother you?"

"Yes, it bothers me. It bothers me that I was so foolish!"

We stepped into the sunshine—blinding for both of us.

"It's very glary after sitting in the dark," Becky commented as she put on her sunglasses. She looked up at me, relieved. "I don't think you're a vampire."

"What was I thinking? Alexander is so special. Why am I acting like Trevor?"

We both stared into the sunshine.

"I had gotten totally caught up in the rumor mill. Just like all the Dullsvillians. I'm no better than they are, am I? We wear different clothes, but I'm just as shallow as they are," I said, disappointed in myself.

"But you wanted him to be a vampire because you like vampires!"

"Thanks. Maybe I'm supposed to give it twenty-four hours," I said as we started to walk home.

I awoke to another sunny day. Not only didn't the sun burn my skin on contact, but its warmth actually felt good against my flesh. Not only didn't mirrors shatter like they did for Gary Oldman in *Bram Stoker's Dracula*, but my reflection looked like it did every day—a pale girl in all black. And the only thing I was thirsty for was a chocolate soda from Shirley's Bakery.

Still, my heart raced when my mother served linguini with garlic for dinner that night. Everyone stared at me as I played with my food, smelling and taking deep breaths.

"What's with you?" Billy Boy asked. "You're acting strange, even for you."

I twirled some pasta on my fork and raised it slowly to my mouth. "Here goes," I said.

My parents looked at me like I was an alien. The noodles touched my tongue and I chewed and chewed and took a huge swallow.

"Here goes what?" my mother asked.

I took a breath. I expected my throat to burn and my skin to crawl. I expected to choke and gasp at the first taste of garlic. And then it happened. Nothing. Nothing is what happened.

"Here's to what?" my mother repeated.

"Here's to . . . here's to another Sarah Madison gourmet dinner!"

Though I wasn't melting in the sun, shattering mirrors, or cringing from the sent of garlic, I was feeling Alexander's power in different ways. I was walking on air, as if I could fly like a bat. I couldn't possibly sleep at night, my mind was racing, dreaming of him, replaying his kisses over and over. I doodled our names surrounded by hearts in all my notebooks during class. I wanted to be with him every moment, because whatever he was, he was my Alexander. My funny, intelligent, caring, lonely, gorgeous, dreamy Alexander. He was more incredible and exceptional than I had ever imagined.

And I was glad I was changing, and not in the way I had fantasized about for so long. I was happy to see my mirrors didn't shatter, because now I saw a reflection of a girl in love, glowing with happiness. Why should I want to live in a cemetery for eternity, when it might be possible to live in Alexander's attic room? I didn't want to cringe from the sunlight but watch Hawaiian sunsets with him. I didn't want to drink blood but sip pop from Alexander's neon-green glasses. I wanted to enjoy the things I had always enjoyed—ice cream, horror movies, swings after dark—but now I wanted to share them with him.

"I heard you're hanging with the vampire," Trevor said the day before the Snow Ball as Becky and I walked through the hall after lunch. Signs for the dance hung from the ceiling and were plastered on the walls. "Isn't it enough that you're a freak and Becky is a troll? Now you have to date a lunatic? Don't you know that the Mansion is haunted?"

"You don't know anything! You've never even met Alexander."

"Oh, Alexander. The monster has a name. I thought you just called him Frankenstein. If I do ever meet him, I'll kick his ass and run him out of town. We need to know that we can walk the streets safely at night!"

"I'll kick your ass if you ever even come near him. If you ever even look at him."

"If he looks anything like you, I'll need sunglasses to guard against the blinding ugliness."

Principal Smith walked by. "I hope everything is okay with you two. We haven't received a budget for new lockers." Then he put his arm around the jerk and said, "I heard you kicked the winning goal in yesterday's game, Trevor."

They turned away, Principal Smith engaging the reluctant Trevor in jock conversation.

"How did he know I'm seeing Alexander?" I asked Becky, puzzled.

"Uh, I guess people . . . you know how people talk in this town."

"Well, people in this town are stupid."

"Listen, Raven, I have something to tell you," she began in a nervous voice that was even more nervous than her normal nervous voice.

But I was distracted by the signs for the dance. TICKETS ON SALE NOW. SAVE FIVE DOLLARS IF YOU PRE-PURCHASE.

"Tickets? Frig! I didn't know I needed tickets!

Do I get them at TicketMaster? Charge by phone?" I laughed. "That's what happens when you're on the outside, you know?"

"I totally know. The outside gets worse and worse each day."

"Maybe they'll be sold out and we'll have to dance on the school lawn," I joked.

But Becky wasn't laughing.

"Maybe it's best you and Alexander have a private dance at the Mansion."

"And miss seeing Trevor's face when I walk in with Alexander?"

"Trevor knows a lot, Raven," she said oddly.

"Fine, so he'll get into a good college. What do I care?"

"I'm afraid of Trevor. His father owns half our farm."

"The corn or the sugar?"

"I have a confession—"

"Save it for Sunday. Forget about Trevor. He's just a bully."

"I'm not strong like you. I never was. You're my best friend, but Trevor has a way of making people say things they don't want to. But please— don't go to the dance," she said, grabbing my arm.

Suddenly the bell rang. "I've gotta go. I can't get another detention or I'll be banned from the dance."

"But Raven—"

"Don't be afraid, girlie, I'll protect you from the monsters."

19

The Snow Ball

I couldn't sit still through the rest of my classes. Not through algebra, history, geography, or English, which I spent underneath the football bleachers composing love poems to Alexander. I raced home and danced around my bedroom. I tried on every piece of clothing I owned in a million combinations until I had the perfect ensemble.

"Are you okay?" Billy Boy asked, peeking his head into my room.

"Just jumping around and dancing, my most precious little brother," I glowed, giving him a big squeeze and a kiss on the head.

"Are you insane?"

I sighed deeply. "You'll understand someday. You'll meet someone who is connected with you in your soul. And then everything will be exciting and peaceful at the same time."

"You mean like Pamela Anderson?"

"No, like a computer-math girl."

Billy Boy gazed off into the distance. "I guess that won't be so bad, as long as she looks like Pamela!"

"She'll look even better!" I said, messing up his hair. "Now get out. I have a ball to attend."

"You're going to a dance?"

"Yes."

"Well . . ." I could see he was revving up for a big sister major put-down. "Well . . . you'll be the prettiest one there."

"Are you sure you're not on drugs?"

"You'll be the prettiest one there . . . with black lipstick."

"Now that sounds more like your style."

I finally paraded into the kitchen, wearing high-heeled knee-high vinyl boots, black fishnet stockings, a black miniskirt, a lacy black tank top, and metallic black bracelets. A black cashmere scarf hid my love bite, and black leather finger-less gloves revealed my black nail polish—glittering like black ice, in keeping with the theme of the Snow Ball.

"Where do you think you're going dressed like that?" my mom asked.

"I'm going to a dance."

"With Becky?"

"No, with Alexander."

"Who's Alexander?"

"The love of my life!"

"What's this I hear about love?" my dad asked, entering the kitchen. "Raven, where are you going dressed like that?"

"She says she's going to a dance with the love of her life," my mom said.

"You're going nowhere in that! And who's the love of your life? A boy from school?"

"Alexander Sterling," I proclaimed.

"As in, the Sterlings that live in the Mansion?" my dad asked.

"The one and only!"

"Not the Sterling boy!" my mom said, shocked. "I've heard horror stories about him! He hangs out at cemeteries and is never seen in the light of day, like a vampire."

"Do you think I'd be going to a dance with a vampire?"

They both stared at me strangely and said nothing.

"Don't be like everyone else in this town!" I shouted.

"Honey, I've heard the stories all over town!" my mom gossiped. "Just yesterday, Natalie Mitchell was saying—"

"Mom, who are you going to believe, me or Natalie Mitchell? This night is very important. It's Alexander's first dance, too. He's so dreamy and intelligent! He knows about art and culture and—"

"Cemeteries?" my dad asked.

"He's not like what people say! He's the most fantabulous guy in our solar system—besides you, Dad."

"Well, in that case, have fun."

"Paul!"

"But not in that outfit," my dad quickly demanded. "Sarah, I'm glad she's going to a dance. Raven's actually going to school without being forced. This is the most normal thing she's done lately."

My mom glared at him.

"But not in that outfit," he repeated.

"Dad, this is all the rage in Europe!"

"But we're not in Europe. We're in a quiet little town where turtlenecks are the rage. Buttoned-up collars, long sleeves, and long skirts."

"No way!" I declared.

"This boy hasn't been out of his room in years, and you're going to let him escort your daughter looking like that?" my mom asked. "Paul, do something."

My father went to the closet. "Here, wear this," he said, handing me one of his sports coats. "It's black."

I stared at him in disbelief.

"It's this or my black bathrobe," he said.

I reluctantly grabbed the coat.

"And we'll be meeting the most fantabulous guy in the solar system when he comes to pick you up?" my mother chimed in.

"Are you kidding?" I was stunned. "Of course not!"

"It's only right, we didn't even know you were seeing him. We had no idea you were going to a dance."

"You want to interrogate and embarrass him. Not to mention me."

"That's what dating is all about. If your date can stand the questions and the parental embarrassment, then he's all yours," my dad teased.

"It's not fair! Do you want to come with us, too?"

"Yes," they both replied.

"This is hideous! It's the biggest night of my life, and you're going to ruin it!"

I heard a car pulling into the driveway. "He's here!" I screamed, peering out the window. "You guys have to be cool!" I said, running around frantically. "Channel those hippie days for me, please! Think about love beads and Joni Mitchell. Think bell-bottoms and incense, not golf pants and china," I begged. "And nothing about cemeteries!"

I wanted this night to be perfect, like it was my wedding day. But I felt like a bride who suddenly wished she had eloped.

Now that my parents were going to meet my

date, my hands began to shake. I was hoping he wouldn't freak out sitting on their perky pastel furniture.

When the doorbell rang, I dashed to greet him. Alexander looked amazing. He was wearing a glossy, chic black three-piece suit and a red silk tie. He looked like one of the billion-dollar basketball players that I see on television interviews. He held a box wrapped in flowered paper.

"Wow!" he said, looking me over. My father nodded to me to put on the sports coat with a scolding eye. Instead I draped it over a chair.

"I should have worn a knit hat or snow boots," he said awkwardly. "I didn't really keep with the theme."

"Forget it! You'll be the best-looking guy there," I complimented, pulling him into the living room. "These are my parents, Sarah and Paul Madison."

"It's wonderful to meet both of you," Alexander said nervously, extending his hand.

"We've heard so much about you." My mother glowed, taking his hand.

I gave her a cold stare.

"Please sit down," she went on. "Would you

like something to drink?"

"No, thank you."

"Make yourself comfortable," my dad said, motioning to the sofa, and settled into his beige recliner.

Uh-oh. I'd never had a guy over before. I could feel my dad taking full advantage. The "goals" inquisition. I prayed it went quickly.

"So, Alexander, how are you finding our town?"

"It's been great since I met Raven," he answered politely and smiled at me.

"So how did you two meet since you don't attend school? Raven neglected to tell us that part."

Oh, no! I started to squirm in my chair.

"Well, I guess we just ran into each other. I mean, it was just one of those things, the right place at the right time. Like they say, everything is about timing and luck. And I'd have to say that I have been very lucky since I met your daughter."

My dad glared at him.

"Oh, no, that's not what I meant," Alexander added.

He turned to me, his ghostlike face bright

red. I tried not to laugh.

"What do your parents do exactly? They aren't in town much, are they?"

"My father is an art dealer. He has galleries in Romania, London, and New York."

"That sounds very exciting."

"It's great, but he's never home," Alexander said. "He's always flying around somewhere."

My mom and dad looked at each other.

"Time to go or we'll be late!" I quickly interjected.

"I almost forgot," Alexander said, awkwardly standing up. "Raven, this is for you."

He handed me the flowered box.

"Thank you!" I smiled anxiously and tore it open, revealing a gorgeous red rose corsage. "It's beautiful!" I gave my mom and dad a look of "See? I told you so."

"How lovely!" my mom gushed.

I held the corsage over my heart as Alexander tried to pin it on. He fumbled out of nervousness.

"Ouch!"

"Did I stick you?" he asked.

"My finger got pricked, but it's okay."

He stared intensely at the drop of blood on the tip of my finger.

My mom stepped between us with a tissue she grabbed from the coffee table.

"It's nothing, Mom, just a little blood. I'm okay." I quickly stuck the pricked finger in my mouth.

"We better go," I said.

"Paul!" my mom pleaded.

But my dad knew better. There was nothing he could do. "Don't forget the coat" was all he said.

I grabbed the coat and Alexander's hand and dragged him out the door, afraid my mom would try to ward him off by making the sign of the cross.

We could hear dance music from the parking lot. No red Camaro anywhere. We were safe—for now.

"Don't forget your jacket," Alexander reminded me as I stepped out of the car.

"You'll have to keep me warm." I winked, leaving it on the backseat.

Two cheerleaders dressed for arctic temperatures stared at us with looks of horror.

I led Alexander away and we paused outside the main entrance. Alexander was like a child, inquisitive and nervous. He looked at the building with interest, like he'd never seen a school before.

"We don't have to go inside," I offered.

"No, that's okay," he said, squeezing my fingers.

Two jocks in the hallway stopped talking the instant they saw us and stared.

"You can pick up your eyeballs off the floor now," I said as I led Alexander past the gawkers.

Alexander examined everything: the Snow Ball signs, the bulletin board announcements, the trophy case. He ran his hand against the lockers, touching the cold metal. "It's just like on TV!"

"Haven't you ever been in a school?" I wondered.

"No."

"Gosh! You're the luckiest guy in the world. You never had to eat a school lunch. Your intestines must be in great shape!"

"But if I went here we would have met sooner."

I hugged him close underneath the same Snow Ball banner that Trevor and I had argued beneath the day before.

Monica Havers and Jodie Carter passed us and did a double take. I thought their eyes were going to bulge right out of their pom-pom heads.

I was ready to fight if they said anything. But I could tell by the pressure on my wrist that Alexander wanted me to remain calm. The girls whispered and giggled to themselves and went on their gossipy way toward the gym.

"Here's where I don't learn chemistry," I said, opening the unlocked door to my chemistry lab. "I usually have to sneak into places. This is a breeze."

"By the way, I've always wanted to know why you snuck in—"

"Look at these!" I interrupted, pointing out the beakers on the lab table. "Lots of mysterious potions and explosions, but that wouldn't bother you, right?"

"I love it!" He was holding a beaker like it was a fine wine.

I pushed him into a desk, then wrote his name on the blackboard.

"Does anybody know the symbol for potassium? Raise your hand."

He raised his hand to the ceiling. "I do!"

"Yes, Alexander?"

"K."

"Correct, you pass the whole year!"

"Miss Madison?" he said, raising his hand again.

"Yes?"

"Can you come here for a moment? I think I need some tutoring. Do you think you can help me?"

"But I just gave you an A!"

"It's more along the lines of anatomy."

I stepped over. He pulled me onto his lap and kissed me softly on the mouth.

We heard some giggling girls run past the open door. "We better go," he suggested.

"No, it's okay."

"I don't want you to get expelled. Besides, we have a dance to attend," he said, making us both stand up.

I walked out hand-in-hand with the guy I had the most chemistry with, his name still etched on the blackboard.

As we approached the gym, I could already feel the cold stares. Everyone was looking at Alexander like he had come from another planet and at me like they always looked at me.

Miss Fay, my nosy algebra teacher, was collecting tickets by the door. "I see you arrived at the dance on time, Raven. Too bad you can't do the same for algebra. I've never seen this gentleman at school," she added, scrutinizing Alexander.

"That's because he doesn't go here." Just take the tickets, lady! I skipped the introductions and pulled Alexander inside.

We walked into the Snow Ball. I didn't know if it was because I was with Alexander, or because it was my first dance, but white had never looked so wonderful. Plastic icicles and snowflakes hung from the ceiling, and the floor was covered with powdery snow. Artificial snow softly sprinkled down from the ceiling. Everyone was dressed in shimmering winter dresses or corduroys with sweaters, mittens, scarves, and hats. The blasting air conditioning sent chills through me.

Even the rock band, The Push-ups, fit the theme with their stocking caps and winter boots.

Refreshments were set up underneath the score-board—snow cones, cider, and hot chocolate.

I could hear whispers, laughs, and gasps as we walked past the bundled-up students. The band, too, was looking at us.

"You want to get some hot chocolate before some senior spikes it?" I asked, trying to distract Alexander from all the attention.

"I'm not thirsty," he replied, watching the dancers.

"I thought you said you were always thirsty?"

The band started to play an electric version of "Winter Wonderland."

"Can I have this dance?" I asked, offering my hand.

I smiled with delight as we walked through the powdered snow to the dance floor.

I was in heaven. I had the best date at the Snow Ball—there was no one more gorgeous than Alexander, and he danced like a dream. We forgot that we were outsiders and thrashed our bodies around like regulars in a trendy club. We danced one song after another without stop-ping—"Cold As Ice," "Ice Cream," "Frosty the Snowman."

The band started to sing, "I Melt with You." The gym was spinning as tiny powdered snowflakes gently fell on us. Alexander and I screamed with laughter as we tripped over an inebriated soccer snob who was making a snow angel on the floor. When the music stopped, I squeezed Alexander like mad, like this was our own private dance. But of course, we weren't alone, as a familiar voice reminded me.

"Does the asylum know you've escaped?" Trevor asked, appearing beside Alexander.

I led Alexander to the refreshment table and grabbed two cherry snow cones.

"Does the warden know you're here?" Trevor asked, pursuing us.

"Trevor, go away!" I said, shielding Alexander with my body.

"Oh, is the Bride of Frankenstein having PMS?"

"Trevor, enough!" I couldn't see Alexander's reaction, but I could feel his hands on my shoulders, drawing me back.

"But this is just the beginning, Raven, just the beginning! Don't they have dungeon dancing? You have to actually go to school to come to the dances," he said to Alexander. "But I guess in Hell there are no rules."

"Shut up!" I said. "Don't you have your own date? Or would that be Matt?" I asked sarcastically.

"Very good. She's clever," he said to Alexander. "But not too clever. No, my date is over there," he added, pointing to the entrance.

I looked over and saw Becky nervously standing at the door, dressed in a long pleated skirt, pale pink sweater, and long white socks with loafers.

My heart sank to the floor. I felt sick.

"I've given her a little makeover," Trevor bragged. "And that's not all, baby."

"If you touch her, I'll kill you!" I screamed, lunging for him.

"I haven't touched her, yet. But there's time. The dance has just begun."

"Raven, what's going on?" Alexander demanded, turning me toward him.

Trevor signaled for Becky to come over. She didn't even look at me as she approached us. Trevor grabbed her hand and kissed her softly on the cheek. I cringed all over and felt nauseated.

"Get off her!" I grabbed her hand and tried to pull her away.

"Raven, is this the guy who's been hassling you?" Alexander asked.

"You mean he doesn't know me? He doesn't know about us?" Trevor asked proudly.

"There is no 'us'!" I tried to explain. "I pissed him off because I'm the only girl in school who doesn't think he's hot! So now he won't leave me alone. But Trevor, how dare you involve Becky and Alexander!"

Becky stood with her eyes glued to the floor.

"I think it's time to leave Raven alone, dude," Alexander said.

"Dude? Now I'm the freakoid's pal? We can hang out and play soccer? Sorry but there's a dress code. No fangs and capes. Go back to the cemetery."

"Trevor, enough! I'll kick you right now!" I threatened.

"It's okay, Raven," Alexander said. "Let's go dance."

"Becky, get away from him!" I yelled, not moving. "Becky, say something! Say something already!"

"She's already said something," Trevor announced. "She's said a lot. It's funny how the people in this town talk and can't shut up when their daddy's crops might suddenly catch fire from a dropped cigarette," Trevor said, looking straight at me.

He turned to Alexander. "You'll learn who these rumorholics are sooner than you think!"

I looked at Becky, who was staring at her loafers. "I'm sorry, Raven. I tried to warn you not to come here tonight."

"What's he talking about?" Alexander wondered.

"Let's go," I said.

"I'm talking about vampires!" Trevor declared.

"Vampires!" Alexander exclaimed.

"Shut up, Trevor!"

"I'm talking about gossip!"

"What gossip?" Alexander said. "I came here to be with my girlfriend."

"Girlfriend?" Trevor asked, surprised. "Then it's official. Are you going to spend all of eternity together?"

"Be quiet!" I ordered.

"Tell him why you broke into his house! Tell him what you saw."

"We're outta here!" I said, starting to go. But Alexander didn't move.

"Tell him why you threw yourself at him," Trevor continued.

"Don't say another word, Trevor!"

"Tell him why you went to the cemetery!"

"I said, 'Shut up!'"

"And why you fainted."

"Shut up!"

"And why you look at yourself in the mirror every hour!"

"What's he talking about?" Alexander demanded.

"And tell him about this," he said, thrusting the Polaroids of my bite mark at Alexander.

Alexander grabbed the picture and examined it. "What's this?"

"She used you," Trevor said. "I started a rumor that snowballed. I had everyone in town believing you were a vampire. The funny thing is, your dear, sweet Raven believed the rumors more than anyone!"

"Shut up!" I screamed and threw my melting

snow cone in Trevor's face.

Trevor laughed as the cherry ice dripped down his cheeks. Alexander stared at the picture.

"What's going on?" Mr. Harris asked, running over.

Alexander looked at me in disbelief and confusion. He glanced around helplessly as the gawking crowd waited for his reaction. Then he angrily grabbed my hand and pulled me outside. We left the falling snow and went out into drizzling rain.

"Wait!" Becky shouted, running after us.

"What's going on, Raven?" Alexander demanded, ignoring her. "How does he know you snuck into my house? How does he know about the cemetery? How does he know you fainted? And what's this?" he asked, shoving the Polaroid at me.

"Alexander, you don't understand."

"You never told me why you snuck into my house," he said.

I stared at his lonely, deep, soulful eyes. His innocence. His sense of not belonging. What could I say? I couldn't lie. So I said nothing and just hugged him with all my might.

The photo dropped from his hand. And he pushed me away.

"I want to hear it from you," he demanded.

Tears started to well up. "I went there to disprove the rumors. I wanted to put an end to them! So your family could live in peace."

"So I was just a ghost story to you, that you had to check out?"

"No! No! Becky, tell him it wasn't like that!"

"It wasn't!" Becky exclaimed. "She talks about you all the time!"

"I thought you were different, Raven. But you used me. You're just like everyone else."

Alexander turned away and I grabbed his arm.

"Don't go! Alexander!" I begged. "It's true, I was caught up in the rumors, but when I first saw you, I knew. I've never felt this way about anyone. That's why I did everything else!"

"I thought you liked me for just being myself—not for who you think I might be. Or for something you think you wanted to become."

He ran away.

"Don't go!" I cried. "Alexander—"

But he ignored me. He was gone, back to the solitude of his attic room.

I stormed into the gym. The band was on break, and everyone looked at me in silence as I crossed the floor.

"The end," Trevor announced and started clapping. "The end! And what a wonderful production it all was, if I do say so myself."

"You!" I yelled. Mr. Harris could see I was going for blood and grabbed me from behind. "You are evil incarnate, Trevor!" I screamed, my arms flailing as I tried unsuccessfully to wriggle out of the soccer coach's grasp. "Trevor Mitchell, you are the monster!" I looked at the faces around me. "Can't you see that? You all pushed away the most giving, lovable, gentle, intelligent person in this town while accepting the wickedest, vilest, most evil monster, just because he dresses like you! Trevor's the one who's destroying lives! And you just watch him play soccer and party with him while you cast out an angel because he wears black and is home-schooled!"

Tears streamed down my face, and I ran outside.

Becky ran after me. "I'm sorry, Raven. I'm sorry!" she shouted.

I ignored her and ran all the way to the Mansion, struggling over the slippery gate. Huge moths fluttered around the porch light as I banged the serpent knocker. "Alexander, open up! Alexander, open up!"

Eventually the light went out and the disappointed moths flew away. I sat on the doorstep crying. For the first time in my life I found no comfort in darkness.

20

Game Over

I cried all night and stayed home from school the next day. At noon I ran to the Mansion. I shook the gate until I thought it would fall over. Finally I climbed over and banged the serpent knocker. The attic curtains ruffled, but no one answered.

Back home I called the Mansion and spoke to Jameson, who said Alexander was asleep. "I'll tell him you rang," he said.

"Please tell him I'm sorry!"

I was afraid Jameson hated me as much as Alexander.

I called every hour; each time Jameson and I had the same conversation.

"I'm going to be home-schooled from now on!" I yelled when my mother tried to get me out of bed the next morning. Alexander wasn't taking my calls, and I wasn't taking Becky's. "I'm never going back to school!"

"You'll get over this, dear."

"Would you have gotten over Dad? Alexander's the only person in the universe who understands me! And I messed it all up!"

"No, *Trevor Mitchell* messed it up. You were nice to that young man. He's lucky to have you."

"You think so?" I started to cry mansion-sized tears. "I think I ruined his life!"

My mom sat on the edge of my bed. "He adores you, honey," she comforted, hugging me like I was a crying Billy Boy. I could smell the apricots in her shampooed velvet-chestnut hair and the sweet soft scent of her perfume. I needed my mom now. I needed her to tell me everything would be all right. "I could see how much he adored you when he came to the house," she continued. "It's a shame people talk about him the way they do."

"You were one of those people," I sighed. "And I guess I was, too."

"No, you weren't. You liked him for who he really was."

"I did—I mean, do. I really do. But it's too late now."

"It's never too late. But speaking of late, I'm late! I have to take your father to the airport."

"Call school," I called to her at the door. "Tell them I'm lovesick."

I pulled the covers over my head. I couldn't move until night. I had to see my Alexander, to shake some sense into his pale body. To beg his forgiveness. I couldn't go to the Mansion, and I couldn't break in—he might call the cops this time. There was only one place to go—one other place where he might be.

I climbed into Dullsville's cemetery with a bouquet of daffodils in my backpack. I walked quickly among the tombstones, trying to retrace the steps we had once taken together. I was as excited as I was nervous. I imagined him waiting for me, running up to me, and giving me a huge hug and showering me with kisses.

But then I thought, *Will he forgive me? Was this our first fight—or our last?*

Eventually I found his grandma's monument, but Alexander wasn't there.

I laid the flowers on the grave. My belly hurt, like it was caving in.

Tears started welling up in my eyes.

"Grandma," I said out loud, looking around. But who could hear me? I could shout if I wanted to. "Grandma, I messed up, messed up big time. There is no one in this world more wild about your grandson than I am. Could you please help me? I miss him so much! Alexander believes I think he's so different, and I do think he's different—but from other people, not from me. I love him. Could you help me?"

I waited, looking for a sign, something magical, a miracle—bats flying overhead or a loud thunderclap. Anything. But there was only the sound of crickets. Maybe it takes a little bit longer for miracles and signs. I could only hope.

One day of being lovesick turned into two days, which turned into three and four.

"You can't make me go to school!" I shouted every morning and turned over and went back to sleep.

Jameson continued to tell me Alexander couldn't come to the phone. "He needs time," Jameson offered. "Please be patient."

Patient? How could I be patient when every second of our separation felt like an eternity?

Saturday morning I had an unwelcome visitor. "I challenge you to a duel!" my father said, throwing his tennis racket on my bed. He opened the curtains and allowed the sun to blind me.

"Go away!"

"You need exercise." He threw a white T-shirt and white tennis skirt onto my bed. "These are Mom's! I didn't think I'd find anything white in your drawers. Now let's scoot! Court time is in half an hour."

"But I haven't played in years!"

"I know. That's why I'm taking you. I want to win today," he said and closed the door behind him.

"You think you'll win!" I yelled through the closed door.

Dullsville's country club was just as I remembered it from all those years ago—snobby and boring. The pro shop was filled with designer tennis skirts and socks, neon balls, and overpriced rackets. There was a four-star restaurant that charged five dollars for a glass of water. I almost fit in, with my mom's white threads, except for the black lipstick. But my father let it go. I think he was happy I was in an upright position.

I ran after my dad's shots with a vengeance, each ball having Trevor Mitchell's face on it. I hit the balls as hard as I could, and naturally they either crashed into the net or into the fence.

"You used to let me win," I said after we ordered lunch.

"How can I let you win when you're slamming every shot into the net? Swing easy and follow through."

"I guess I've been hitting the ball in the wrong direction a lot lately. I never should have let Trevor get the best of me. I should never have believed the rumors, or wanted to believe them. I miss Alexander so much."

At lunch the waiter brought me a garden salad and a tuna melt for my dad. I stared at my tomatoes, eggs, and romaine lettuce. "Dad, do you think I'll ever meet someone like Alexander again?"

"What do you think?" he asked, taking a bite of his sandwich.

"I don't think I will. I think he's it. He's the special one people only find in movies and gushy romance novels. Like Heathcliff or Romeo."

My eyes welled up with tears.

"It's okay, honey," he said, handing me his napkin. "When I met your mother, I wore John Lennon glasses and had hair down to the middle of my back. I didn't know what a pair of scissors or a razor looked like! Her father didn't like me because of the way I looked and my radical politics. But she and I saw the world the same way. And that's all that mattered. It was a Wednesday when I first saw your mom, on the university lawn, in maroon bell-bottoms and a white halter top, twirling her long brown hair, gazing up. I walked over and asked what she was staring at. 'That mother bird is feeding its baby birds. Isn't it beautiful?' she said. 'It's a raven!' And she quoted some lines from Edgar Allan Poe. I laughed. 'What are you laughing at?' she asked me. And I told her it was a crow, not a raven. 'Oh, that's what I get for partying too hard last night,' she said, laughing with me. 'But aren't they beautiful just the same?' And I told her right there and then that yes, they were. But she was more beautiful."

"You said that?"

"I shouldn't be telling you this. Especially the part about the partying!"

"Mom always told me that's how I got my name, but she never mentioned the partying."

I thanked the universe my parents had been looking at a raven that day and not a squirrel. The results would have been disastrous.

"Dad, what do I do?"

"You'll have to figure that one out yourself. But if the ball lands in your court again, don't smash it into the fence. Just open your eyes and swing right through."

We got my salad to go as I couldn't chew on it and the tennis metaphors at the same time.

I was greatly confused. I didn't know what to do. Hit the ball or wait for it to come to me? My father was lollygagging with a friend when I heard a voice say, "You play a mean game, Raven!" I turned around and saw Matt leaning against the front counter.

"I can't play at all!" I replied, surprised. I looked around for Trevor.

"I'm not talking about tennis."

"I don't understand."

"I'm talking about school, about Trevor. Don't worry, he's not here."

"So, are you trying to start something with me?" I asked, clutching my racket. "Here at the club?"

"No, I'm trying to end it. I mean, what he does to you and Becky and everyone. Even me. And I'm his best friend. But you stick up for everyone here. And you don't even like us." He laughed. "We're mean to you and you still get Trevor back for all of us."

"Are we on *Spy TV*?" I asked, looking around for hidden cameras.

"You bring spice to this town, with your funky clothes and your attitude. You don't care what people think, and this town revolves on what people think."

"Is Trevor hiding in the gift shop?" I asked, peering over.

"The Snow Ball really changed a lot of people's minds. Trevor used the whole school, and in the end he made fools of everyone. I think it was our wake-up call."

I realized there were no hidden cameras or hiding Trevors. Matt wasn't joking.

"I wish Alexander could hear you say this," I finally said. "I haven't seen him, and I'm afraid I never will again. Trevor ruined everything," I said, my eyes starting to well up again.

"Screw Trevor!"

Several people looked over, as it wasn't polite to swear at the club, even though they did on the court after they missed a shot.

"Gotta run, Raven—see you," Matt said as he took off.

"I'd like you to meet an old acquaintance, Raven," my father said, approaching with a strikingly suntanned man after Matt left.

"It's nice to see you, Raven," he said. "It's been a while. You look so grown-up now. I wouldn't recognize you without the lipstick. Do you remember me?"

How could I forget him? The first time I entered the Mansion, the basement window, the red cap. The warm kiss on my cheek from the handsome new guy trying to fit in.

"Jack Patterson! Of course I remember you, but I can't believe you remember me."

"I'll always remember you!"

"How do you two know each other?" my father asked.

"From school," Jack answered, with a glint in his eye.

"So what are you up to now?" Jack asked me. "Rumor has it that you're going into the Mansion through the front door these days."

"Well, I was, but . . ."

"Jack recently moved back to town and took over his father's department store," my dad said.

"Yeah, stop by sometime," Jack said. "I'll give you a discount."

"Do you sell combat boots and black cosmetics?"

Jack Patterson laughed. "I guess some things haven't changed!"

Matt suddenly returned. "Ready to go, Matt?" Jack asked.

"You know Matt?" I asked, surprised.

"We're cousins. I'm glad I moved back—I have some reservations about the crowd he hangs around with."

21

Darkness and Light

I t was Saturday evening. I was dressed in my Cure T-shirt and black boxers, watching *Dracula* in slow motion. I paused the part where Bela leans into a sleeping Helen Chandler and recalled the time Alexander kissed me on his black leather couch. I stared longingly at the screen and grabbed some more tissues.

The doorbell shocked me out of my self-pitying trance. "You get it!" I shouted, and suddenly remembered my family had gone to the movies.

I peered through the peephole but saw nothing.

Then I looked again and discovered tiny Becky standing on the doorstep.

"What do you want?" I asked, opening the door.

"Get dressed!"

"I thought maybe you came here to apologize."

"I'm sorry, but you must believe me! You have to come to the Mansion—now!"

"Go home!"

"Raven, immediately!

"What's going on?"

"Please, Raven, hurry!"

I ran upstairs and threw on a black T-shirt and black jeans.

"Hurry!"

I ran back downstairs. She grabbed my arm and pulled me out the door.

I bombarded her with questions as we got into her father's pickup, but she refused to tell me anything.

I imagined the Mansion covered with graffiti, its windows shattered, Trevor and his soccer snobs having it out on the hill with a bloody Alexander. And then another horrible image, but a silent one. A FOR SALE sign in the yard and not even the dark curtains hanging in Alexander's attic window.

Becky didn't park at the Mansion, but a block away.

"What gives?" I asked. "Why don't you park closer?"

But as we jumped out, I saw several cars parked along the curb leading up to the Mansion, unusual for the desolate street.

In the distance I spotted two women dressed in black like they were going to a funeral. But they were swiftly walking, holding lighted torches.

My heart sank. "We'll never make it!" I shouted.

Worse still was seeing a man, also dressed in black and carrying a lighted torch. I freaked. Everything stopped inside of me. It was just like the ending of *Frankenstein*—where the townspeople gather to burn the castle and cast out poor Franky from his home. Only this was a smaller mob. I couldn't believe it had come to this. I could already smell the smoke.

"No, no!" I shouted, but the man had already

turned the corner toward the gate.

My darkest imagination could not have prepared me for what I laid my eyes upon: A small
crowd of Dullsvillians had gathered on the
Mansion grounds. Conservative townspeople
dressed in vampire black? Everyone was so dark
I thought I must be wearing sunglasses, but a
glowing Becky convinced me I was seeing a perfect picture. There were lively people hanging
outside the front of the usually lonely
Mansion—and they were all having a blast!

I didn't understand any of it. The gathering
was more like a party, but it made no sense. Was it
just another sick joke? And then I saw the banner
on the open gate that made everything wonderfully clear: WELCOME TO THE NEIGHBORHOOD.

"Better late than never," Becky said.

Red streamers also hung from the gate, and
lawn torches lit the hill.

"Hey, girl, don't ignore us!" someone called
as Becky and I entered the grounds.

I turned around. It was Ruby! She was
dressed in a skin-tight black-vinyl dress, and
thigh-high black-vinyl go-go boots.

"I've gotten a date out of this outfit already,

Raven. You'll never believe it—it was from the butler!" She grimaced like a smitten giggly school girl and fluffed her dyed black hair as she checked herself out in her compact. "He's older, but he's kinda cute!"

By the looks of Ruby, she had been pulled straight off a Paris fashion runway. Even her white poodle was wearing a studded black leash and a black doggie sweater.

"Recognize me?" It was Janice in a black mini and combat boots. "Think it's my color?" she said, revealing her black nail polish.

"Any shade of black will do!" I said.

"I tried to tell you not to come to the Snow Ball," Becky began quickly as we walked up the driveway. "But Trevor blackmailed me. You're always there for me when I need you and I wasn't there for you. Will you ever forgive me?"

"I was so caught up, I didn't listen to your warnings. And you're here for me now." I took her hand. "I'm just glad you're not under Trevor's spell anymore."

As Becky and I continued to walk up the hill of party goers, we ran into Jack Patterson wearing a black turtleneck and jeans.

"I've been waiting all these years for the right moment to pay you back," he confessed. "I've outfitted the party. There's nothing black left in the store!"

Now, after all these years, it was my turn to give him a grateful kiss on the cheek. "This is so unbelievable!"

"It wasn't my idea for the partiers to wear black," Jack said, pointing to a guy in Doc Martens, a black T-shirt, and slicked-back hair.

"Hey, girl!" It was Matt. "I was afraid you wouldn't show. We had to send Becky for you. We couldn't properly welcome Alexander to town after all this time without you!" My eyes lit up. "Alexander's been asking about you all night."

I glanced around frantically, speechless. I wanted to throw my arms around everyone. But where was Alexander?

"I think you'll find him inside," Matt hinted.

"I can't believe you did this!" The thought of seeing Alexander again thrilled me. I gave Matt a Ruby squeeze-hug. I think he was as startled by my affection as I was.

"You better get up there—before the sun rises," he said.

I paused, remembering one Dullsvillian I hadn't spotted. "He's not going to be lurking in the shadows, right?"

"Who?"

"You know who!"

"Trevor? He wasn't invited."

"Thanks, Matt. Thank you so much!" I said, giving him a thumbs-up.

"You did this, really. It's been good for us to take a walk on the wild side."

Becky grabbed my arm and led me toward the Mansion. A refreshment table was set up by the door. Juices and pop, chips and SnoCaps, Sprees, Good & Plenty, and Dots. Everything that Alexander had that night we watched TV at his house.

"No way!" I exclaimed. I glared at Becky. "I even told you about the SnoCaps?" I realized.

"If I kept that a secret, too, we wouldn't have refreshments," Becky added.

She prepared herself for my fury, but instead I smiled and said, "I'm glad you have such a good memory. Whose idea was this welcome party?" I wondered.

Becky glanced toward the front steps.

Out of the corner of my eye I noticed two trendy honeymooners holding hands.

"Oh, there she is," I heard the hipster man say.

It was my parents! My mom was in black bell-bottoms, black platform sandals, and a silky black shirt, with a string of red love beads around her neck. My dad was wearing black-rimmed John Lennon glasses and had squeezed his body into black Levi's and a black silk shirt unbuttoned halfway.

"Are you on drugs?" I wondered aloud, astonished.

"Hi, honey," my mom said. "We had to do something to get you out of bed."

My dad laughed and two young kids in Dracula outfits came whizzing by. One extended his cape with his hands and pretended to fly toward me.

"I've come to suck your blood!" It was Billy Boy.

"You look divine! You're the cutest vampire I've ever seen," I said.

"Really? Then I'm going to wear this to school on Monday."

"Oh, no, you're not," my dad scolded. "One radical in the family is more than I can handle."

My father looked at my mother for help. Billy winked at me and flew off.

Jameson stepped out of the Mansion holding a black jacket.

"Here is your sports coat, Mr. Madison," he said, handing the jacket to my dad. "The boy wouldn't let it go. Something about your daughter's perfume."

I was totally embarrassed, but I melted inside.

"It's good to see you, Miss Raven."

I wanted to see Alexander. I wanted to see him right then. I wanted to see his face, his hair, his eyes. I wanted to see if he still looked the same, if he still felt our deep love connection. Or if he thought it was all a lie.

As if he could read my thoughts, Jameson said, "Won't you come in?"

I walked inside, thankful that the reunion—or the blowout—would be a private one. It was quiet inside, no music pulsing from the attic, and dark, with only a few candles lighting the way. I checked the living room, the dining room, the kitchen and the hallway. I climbed the grand staircase.

"Alexander?" I whispered. "Alexander?"

My heart was pounding and my mind frenetic. I peeked in the bathrooms, the library, the master bedroom.

I heard voices from the TV room.

Renfield was ratting to the doctor about Count Dracula. It was during this scene that Alexander had kissed me and I had fainted. I sat on the couch and watched impatiently for a minute, expecting him to return. But I grew anxious and wandered back out to the hallway.

"Alexander?"

I looked at the faded red-carpeted staircase leading to the attic. His staircase!

The door at the top of his squeaky stairs was closed. His door. His room. The room he wouldn't let me see. I gently knocked on the door.

No answer. "Alexander?" I knocked again. "It's me, Raven. Alexander?"

Behind that door was his world. The world I had never seen. The world that had all the answers to all his mysteries—how he spent his days, how he spent his nights. I twisted the knob, and the door creaked slightly open. It wasn't locked. I wanted more than anything to push it open. To snoop. But then I thought. This is how the trouble began: with my snooping. Haven't I learned anything? So I took a deep breath and acted against my impulse. I shut the door and hurried down the creaky attic stairs and the grand staircase with a new confidence. I paused at the open front door, and feeling a familiar presence once again, I turned around.

There he stood, like a Knight of the Night, looking straight at me with those dark, deep, lovely, calming, lonely, adoring, intelligent, dreamy, soulful eyes.

"I never meant to hurt you," I blurted out. "I'm not what Trevor said. I've always liked you, for who you are!"

Alexander didn't speak.

"I was so stupid. You're the most interesting thing that's ever happened in Dullsville. You must think I'm so childish."

He still didn't speak a word.

"Say something. Say I was totally third grade. Say you hate me."

"I know we are more similar than different."

"You do?" I asked, surprised.

"My grandma told me."

"She speaks to you?" I said, feeling a sudden chill.

"No, she's dead, silly! I saw the flowers."

He reached his hand for mine. "There's something I want to show you," he said mysteriously.

"Your room?" I asked, grabbing his hand.

"Yes, and something in my room. It's finally ready."

"It?" My imagination ran wild. What did Alexander do up in his room? Was "it" alive or dead?

He led me up the grand staircase and the creaky attic stairs. His stairs.

"It's time you knew my secrets," he said, opening the door. "Or at least most of them."

It was dark except for the moonlight that shone through the tiny attic window. A beat-up, comfy chair and a twin-sized mattress rested on the floor. A strewn black comforter exposed maroon sheets. A bed like any other teenager's. Not a coffin. And then I noticed the paintings. Big Ben with bats flying over the clock face, a castle on a hill, the Eiffel Tower upside down.

There was a dark painting of an older couple in gothic outfits with a huge red heart around them. There was Dullsville's cemetery, his grandma smiling above her gravestone. A picture drawn from his attic window with trick-or-treaters everywhere. "Those are from my dark period," he joked.

"They're spectacular," I said, stepping closer.

Paint was everywhere, even splattered on the floor.

"You're totally awesome!"

"I wasn't sure you'd like them."

"They're unbelievable!"

I noticed a canvas covered with a sheet on an easel in the corner.

"Don't worry, it won't bite."

I paused before it, wondering what lay beneath the sheet. And for once my imagination failed me. I took a corner of the sheet and slowly peeled it back, just like when I had uncovered the mirror in Alexander's basement. I was stunned.

I was staring at myself, dressed for the Snow Ball, a red rose corsage pinned to my dress. But I carried a pumpkin basket over my arm and held a Snickers in one hand while on the other I wore a spider ring. Stars twinkled overhead and snow fell lightly around me. I grinned wonderfully through glistening fake vampire teeth.

"It looks just like me! I never imagined you were an artist! I mean I knew you did those drawings in the basement and then the paint on the side of the road . . . I had no idea."

"That was you?" he asked, reflecting.

"Why were you standing in the middle of the road?"

"I was going to the cemetery to paint this picture of my grandmother's monument."

"Don't most painters use little tubes?"

"I mix my own."

"I had no idea. You're an artist. Now it all makes sense. "

"I'm glad you like it," he said with relief. "We better get back to the party before we give them something to really gossip about."

"I guess you're right. You know how rumors spread in this town."

"Isn't it weird?" he asked, handing me a soda, back on the lawn after we'd mingled among the darkened Dullsvillians. "We're not the outcasts tonight."

"Let's enjoy it now. It'll all be back to normal tomorrow."

The party goers were smiling and having fun.

But then I noticed a figure in the distance slowly running up the driveway.

"Trevor!" I said, with a gasp. "What's he doing here?"

"He's a monster!" he yelled, approaching the party. "His whole family."

"Not this again!" I said.

All eyes were on Trevor.

"Alexander, go back inside," I urged. But he didn't move.

"He hangs out in the cemetery for freakin' sake!" Trevor said, pointing to my Gothic Mate. "There were no bats in this town before he came!" he shouted.

"And there weren't losers in this town before you came!" I said.

"Raven, calm down," my father admonished sternly.

"Enough of this!" Matt said, bursting forth,

with Jack Patterson right behind him.

"Look here! I've been attacked!" Trevor exclaimed, pointing to a scratch on his neck. "By a bat! I'm going to have to get freakin' rabies shots!"

"Let it go, Trevor," Matt said, exhausted.

"It happened on the way here. I'd called your house and your mom said you were partying at freak Mansion. What's up with that? You were suppossed to be hanging out with me!"

"You've done this to yourself," Matt answered. "I'm through driving you around town so you can spread your stupid rumors. You've played me long enough, Trev."

"But I was right! They are vampires!" Trevor shouted.

"And I was right when I didn't invite you," Matt said.

"You guys are crazy. Partying with freaks!" Trevor argued, glaring at us all.

"Okay, Trevor, that's enough," my father said, stepping toward him.

"I didn't have anything to do with this," Alexander said, confused.

"I think we know that," I confirmed.

"But—" Trevor began, his angry eyes thirsting for blood.

"I'd rather not have to call your father," my dad finally said, putting his hand on Trevor's shoulder.

Trevor was fuming, but he was running out of steam. There was no one here who'd fall for his jokes, take his side, think he was wonderful for scoring a winning goal. No giggling girls who wanted to date a soccer snob or hang with him anymore because he was popular. There was nothing left for him to do but leave.

"You just wait—my dad owns this town!" he said, as he stormed off. It was the only thing he could say.

"Don't forget to use some ice on that," my mom advised as if she were Florence Nightingale.

"He needs a tranquilizer gun, not ice, Mom."

We all watched as Trevor reached the gate and was finally gone.

"Well, we had planned on a singing telegram, but they must have gotten the instructions wrong," my dad joked. The crowd laughed with relief.

Alexander and I hung onto each other for comfort. The children began running around, pretending to be vampires.

Later, after Alexander had said good-bye to his neighbors, Becky found me cleaning up the refreshment table.

"I'm sorry," she said.

"Are you going to apologize for the rest of your life?"

I gave her a Ruby squeeze-hug. "See you tomorrow," Becky said with tired eyes.

"I thought your parents already left."

"They keep farm hours, you know. Early to bed and early to rise."

"Then who are we riding with?" I asked, confused.

"Matt."

"Matt!"

She smiled an I-have-a-crush smile. "He's not as snobby as he seems."

"I know. Who would have thought?"

"He's never ridden on a tractor before," Becky said. "Do you think he says that to every girl?"

"No, Becky, I think he really means it!"

"C'mon, Becky," Matt called, just like he used to call Trevor.

"I'll catch up in a minute," I said.

I was helping Jameson with the last of the party trash when Alexander descended the stairs, wearing a cape, slicked-back hair, and fake vampire teeth.

"My dream vampire," I said.

He pulled me close in the hallway.

"You tried to save me tonight," he said. "I will be eternally grateful."

"Eternally," I said with a grin.

"Hopefully someday I'll return the favor."

I giggled as he nibbled on my neck. "I don't want to go," I whined. "But Becky is waiting. See you tomorrow?" I asked. "Same bat time? Same bat channel?"

He walked me to the door and playfully bit me on the neck with his vampire teeth.

I laughed and tried to pull the fake teeth out of his mouth.

"Ouch," he exclaimed.

"You're not supposed to Superglue them on!"

"Raven, you don't still believe in vampires, do you?" he asked.

"I think you've cured me of that," I answered. "But I'm going to keep the black lipstick."

He gave me a long, heavenly good-night kiss.

As I turned to leave, I noticed Ruby's monogrammed compact on the doorstep and picked it up. I opened it to smooth out my lipstick. I saw the Mansion's open door reflected in its glass.

"Sweet dreams," I heard Alexander say.

But he didn't appear in the mirror.

I turned around. Alexander was clearly standing in the doorway.

But when I checked the mirror again, he was gone!

When I turned around once again, I found the serpent door knob staring me in the face. I rapped on it desperately.

"Alexander! Alexander!"

I backed away from the door in disbelief. I slowly retreated and stared up at the attic window. The light came on.

"Alexander!" I called.

He peered out from behind the ruffled

curtains, my Gothic Guy, my Gothic Mate, my Gothic Prince, my Knight of the Night. Looking down at me, longingly. He touched the window with the palm of his hand. I stood motionless. As I began to reach toward him, he withdrew from the curtain and the light vanished.

My childhood dream had come true, but it was more of a nightmare than I could have imagined. I lay awake all night, trying to make sense of it all.

The guy I was in love with was really a vampire? Would I spend eternity as a cool ghoul?

I didn't react to this development in the way I'd always dreamed. I didn't pick up the phone to call CNN. In fact, the whole ride home with Becky I didn't say a word, only stared out the window in disbelief as she flirted with Matt.

At home I locked myself in my bedroom. I

scoured my vampire books for answers but found none. I rehearsed telling him that I loved him, no matter who or what he was. That his secret was safe with me. But was I prepared to leave everything I knew? Trade my world for his? Leave my parents? Becky? Even Billy Boy? I stared at my reflection in the full-length mirror, as if for the last time.

I spent the next day at the cemetery, pacing in front of the baroness's monument. As soon as the sun set behind the trees, I took off for the Mansion.

When I came around the hill, I noticed the gate was locked. I scaled the fence to find the Mansion even more eerie and lonely than usual. The Mercedes was gone and the lights were off. I rang the bell, over and over. I rapped on the serpent knocker. No one answered. I peered through the living room window. White sheets were draped over the furniture. I ran around back and pressed my nose against the basement window. I couldn't breathe. The crates of earth were no longer there!

My heart sank. I couldn't swallow.

I reached for the loose brick I had formerly used to sneak in. But when I pulled on it, an envelope with my name written across it in large letters fell out.

I raced to the front gate and held the letter under the light.

I saw my name clearly.

I pulled out a black card. In blood-red letters were four simple words: BECAUSE I LOVE YOU.

I caressed the words with my fingertips and held the letter to my heart. Tears fell from my face as I wearily slunk against the Mansion gate.

It was a stake shoved into my heart.

Birds chirped overhead and I looked up to see them hovering over the trees. One swooped down and landed above me on the iron gate.

It was a bat.

Its wings remained solemnly still as it fixed its gaze upon me. Its shadow prominent on the pavement, its breath in time with mine. Bats are blind, but this one seemed to be staring right into my soul.

I slowly reached for it. "Alexander?"

And then it flew away.

ACKNOWLEDGMENTS

A million thanks to my editor, Katherine Brown Tegen, for your experienced advice, talent, and friendship.

Many thanks to Julie Hittman, for your hard work and communication, and the wonderful staff at HarperCollins.

I'm deeply grateful to my brother, Mark Schreiber, for your generosity and expertise.

XOXO to Suzie, Ben, and Audrey Schreiber, for your support and the memorable trip to New Orleans.

Read on for a preview of the
exciting sequel to Vampire Kisses:

Kissing
Coffins

It was like a final nail in a coffin.

Becky and I were camped out in my darkened bedroom, engrossed in the eighties cult horror classic *Kissing Coffins*. The femme fatale, Jenny, a teenage, malnourished blond wearing a size negative-two white cotton dress, was desperately running up a serpentine rock footpath toward an isolated haunted mansion. Bright veins of lightning shot overhead in the pouring rain.

Only the night before had Jenny unearthed the true identity of her fiancé when she stumbled upon his hidden dungeon and found him climbing out of a coffin. The dashing Vladimir Livingston, a renowned English professor, was not a mere mortal after all, but an immortal blood-sucking vampire. Upon hearing Jenny's blood-curdling screams, Professor Livingston immediately covered his fangs with his black cape. His red eyes remained unconcealed, gazing back at her longingly.

"You cannot bear witness to me in this state," I said along with the vampire.

Jenny didn't flee. Instead, she reached out toward her fiancé. Her vampire love growled, reluctantly stepped back into the shadows, and disappeared.

The fang flick had gathered a goth cult following that continued today. Audience members flocked to retro cine-mas in full costume, shouted the lines of the movie in unison, and acted out the various roles in front of the screen. Although I'd seen the movie a dozen times at home on DVD and knew all the words, I'd never been blessed with participating in a theatrical showing. This was Becky's first time watching it. We sat in my room, glued to the screen, as Jenny decided to return to the professor's mansion to confront her immortal lover. Becky dug her gnawed-on blood-red-painted fingernails into my arm as Jenny slowly opened the creaky wooden arch-shaped dungeon door. The ingénue softly crept down the massive winding staircase into Vladimir's darkened basement, torches and cobwebs hanging on the cement brick walls. A simple black coffin sat in the center of the room, earth sprinkled beneath it. She approached it cautiously. With all her might, Jenny lifted the heavy coffin lid.

Violins screeched to a climax. Jenny peered inside. The coffin was empty.

Becky gasped. "He's gone!"

Tears began to well in my eyes. It was like watching myself on-screen. My own love, Alexander Sterling, had vanished into the night two evenings ago, shortly after I had discovered he, too, was a vampire.

Jenny leaned over the empty casket and melodramatically wept as only a B-movie actress could.

A tear threatened to fall from my eye. I wiped it off with the back of my hand before Becky could see. I pressed the "Stop" button on the remote and the screen went black.

"Why did you turn it off?" Becky asked. Her disgruntled face was barely illuminated by the few votives I had scattered around my room. A tear rolling down her cheek caught the reflection of one of the candles. "It was just getting to the good part."

"I've seen this a hundred times," I said, rising, and ejected the DVD.

"But *I* haven't," she whined. "What happens next?"

"We can finish it next time," I reassured her as I put the DVD away in my closet.

"If Matt were a vampire," Becky pondered, referring to her khaki-clad new boyfriend, "I'd let him take a bite out of me anytime."

I felt challenged by her innocent remark, but I bit my tongue. I couldn't share my most secretest of secrets even with my best friend.

"Really, you don't know what you'd do" was all I could say.

"I'd let him bite me," she replied matter-of-factly.

"It's getting late," I said, turning on the light.

I hadn't slept the last two nights since

Alexander left. My eyes were blacker than the eye shadow I put on them.

"Yeah, I have to call Matt before nine," she said, glancing at my *Nightmare Before Christmas* alarm clock. "Would you and Alexander meet us for a movie tomorrow?" she asked, grabbing her jean jacket from the back of my computer chair.

"Uh . . . we can't," I stalled, blowing out the votives. "Maybe next week."

"Next week? But I haven't even seen him since the party."

"I told you, Alexander's studying for exams."

"Well, I'm sure he'll ace them," she said. "He's been cracking the books all day and night."

Of course, I couldn't tell anyone, even Becky, why Alexander had disappeared. I wasn't even sure of the reason myself.

But mostly, I couldn't admit to myself that he had gone. I was in denial. *Gone*—the word turned my stomach and choked my throat. Just the thought of explaining to my parents that Alexander had left Dullsville brought tears to my eyes. I couldn't bear accepting the truth, much less telling it.

Sink your teeth into this suspenseful sequel

Hc 0-06-077622-6

The story of the extraordinary romance between Raven and Alexander continues as Raven learns that love always has its complications. When Alexander disappears, Raven must embark on a dangerous search—one that may change her life forever. Raven will face a life-transforming decision: Should she become a vampire?

Katherine Tegen Books
An Imprint of HarperCollinsPublishers

www.harperteen.com

Also by Ellen Schreiber

Hc 0-06-009338-2

Hc 0-06-008204-6

Comedy Girl

When Trixie Shapiro wins a spot at the comedy club, it's the start of a dream come true. But as her career begins, she's falling in love with her longtime crush. When her two worlds compete, Trixie must choose between romance and a risky shot at fame.

"Trixie will keep her audience amused, even as she teaches something about the cost—and rewards— of pursuing a dream."   —*Publishers Weekly*

Teenage Mermaid

Spencer is a surfer. He lives near the sea. Lilly is a mermaid. She lives in the sea. The two have a chance encounter when Lilly rescues Spencer from almost drowning in a surfing accident. It's only destiny that they meet again . . . and fall in love.

"A sharp, funny novel that includes a super-sized serving of over-the-top romance."   —ALA *Booklist*

www.harperteen.com   ≡ Katherine Tegen Books
An Imprint of HarperCollinsPublishers